THE REPLACEMENT

Book 1 of The Replacement Series

BIANCA SIERRA-LUEBKE

This is a work of fiction. Names, characters, places, and incidents either are the product of the author's imagination or are used fictitiously, and any resemblance to actual persons, living or dead, business establishments, events, or locales is entirely coincidental.

ISBN 978-1-983-13589-7

This book is dedicated to my mom Eadie.

Over the years, I set this book aside time and again. Life happened and for months, sometimes years, I forgot about it. My mother never forgot. Every so often, she would nudge, asking about the book. Her eyes would turn serious as she reminded me that I was a writer. After a visit to her house two years ago, I left determined to prove her right.

Acknowledgements

For the past two years, I have used nearly all my spare time to finish The Book, as I so often refer to it. Despite being a self-published book, many people helped me along the way. I want to thank them. My beta readers (Bethany, Lupe, Tracy and Mom) for suffering through the rawest draft in the history of writing. The editing party crew (Rik, Cari, Lupe, Chey, Kevin and Mom) for convincing me to change Lymeria to Lymerian, among other things. My children (Isabel and Jeremiah) for understanding every time I locked myself away for hours to write. Finally, I want to thank my husband Kevin, for his constant patience and support.

Chapter 1

Angelica

Two days ago they caught me breaking the law. Not the kind of law that polices our cities or keeps us safe at night—not a human law. I broke a Lymerian law, and now I'm going to die.

I should have listened to Merrick.

This *cell* isn't suited for humans like me. Absent of light or heat, stale air keeps me a prisoner as much as the lock on the door. I never imagined I would miss a painless breath. Too weak to move, yet alive enough to keep forcing air in and out of my suffocating lungs.

"Merrick," I whisper into the uneven stone beneath me. Even now, in this horrific place, I miss him. Growing up in a Catholic orphanage never inspired me to pray—until now. With what little strength I have, I kneel and clasp my hands. They could be listening, so I say the prayer in my head.

Dear God, let Merrick live. Help him find another way to make his dreams come true. Let him be a father. A sob stops in my throat while tears rush down my mud-stained face. I'm not sure what hurts more, imagining him escaping without me, or imagining what they will do to him if they catch him. My stomach spasms, folding my body over on itself. I try to keep upright, but my human needs overpower me. The ache in my stomach is nothing compared to the scorching thirst in my throat, but mostly I need sleep.

Is this seat taken? Merrick's sweet words in my memories keep me company as I drift in and out of wakefulness. The diner near my boarding school, and a boy gesturing to the seat next to me flash beneath my eyelids. Meeting Merrick, this moment, changed my life. We fit together so well it was easy to fall completely in love with him.

Before long, Merrick told me what he was, trying to scare me away, but it backfired. My love deepened, and I vowed to help him, to free him of his unending days on Earth.

But you look like everyone else.

Not all of us look human. Centuries of living on Earth and eating a human diet has made us look alike. Blood works best to change us, our cells. Enough human blood can make us human completely.

I want to help you.

Merrick's deepest desire is to be human. With my help, he would finally age and live a final lifetime . . . with me.

Another day goes by, or so I think. My grasp on reality is slipping as time warps in this place between places—between dreams and reality. I repeat our story so it doesn't slip away with my sanity. *I'm Angelica Franklin and this is Krisenica, the fifth home to the Lymerians living in secret on Earth. It's been one year since I met Merrick. Six months since I knew I could not live without him. Three months since we started to run. Three days since they caught me.*

I begged him to stay or take me with him, not knowing how to live without him. Merrick knew we would be caught if I left with him—he promised it. I wouldn't listen.

You can't go. You can't leave me when we've just met.

I have never met anyone like you, but what I want does not matter. There are rules. Those of us allowed in the human world are here under strict guidelines. They have told me it is time for me to leave.

I want to go too. Help me like I've been helping you.

Even with my blood to make you stronger, the danger of being noticed together is too great. When we are caught, you will not want to die for this.

It was a simple plan: Merrick continues to drink my blood, day by day shedding his Lymerian form for human. I drink his blood to strengthen my limbs as we outrun the Lymerians. Together we find a place they will not follow.

It was a stupid plan.

My eyes sting, but the tears stay put this time. My dehydrated body refuses to risk even a single tear. Despair urges me to wallow in my thirst, but I refuse and focus on Merrick. At least he will live. Even if they find him, they won't kill him. They don't kill their own kind. Is that why he said yes, because his life was never in jeopardy? But no. I scold myself, knowing Merrick loves me, and some punishments are worse than death.

I shudder to remember Merrick's stories that seemed more fiction than reality, which is why I never truly believed them. One tale stands out among the others. Long ago, disobedient Lymerians were bled and imprisoned for decades, left to starve. Starvation cannot kill a Lymerian, but it causes pain. Agonizing pain. Guilt swallows me as I comprehend Merrick's fate if he is found. What have I done?

The screech of metal on metal, the bolt of the door changing direction, jerks me out of these horrid thoughts. Fresh scratches etch into my cheek as I drag my face toward the sound. When the cell door swings open, a faint light illuminates two gigantic forms wearing gray hooded cloaks. The hoods cover their faces, and I imagine grotesque aliens underneath—real Lymerians. One is carrying a canister. *Water*. He rolls it in my direction, the clang of steel on stone terrorizing my ears until it slows to a stop. I stay still until the door booms shut behind them, sounding more like the gateway to a castle instead of a simple cell.

I force weak limbs to move one in front of the other until my fingers feel salvation. One can doesn't even scratch the surface of what my body needs, but I feel a little more alive. In desperation, I leave the canister at my lips, hoping for another drop. The canister slips through my fingers as I startle from the door screeching open again. This time they both enter and each grab an arm.

Something like adrenaline pumps through me, and I thrash and try to yell. It comes out more like a croak. And who am I yelling for? No one can help me now.

"Don't touch me! I can walk on my own," I say, finding my voice. They let me wriggle out of their arms. The two men start walking, and I stumble behind, using the wall to steady myself. It's still too dark for me to see properly, and the air is only slightly easier to breathe. Before long, my starving body gives out. They drag me the rest of the way, taking no care with my fragile human skin. By the time we reach an elevator, my knees and shins are bloody.

We ride much longer than any elevator I've been on. Or maybe it seems that way because I know it's finally time. I'm going to die. Shock sets in, speeding up my pulse and setting my breaths to a quick beat. By the time the elevator stops, I'm a ball on the floor, cowering for my life.

My arms unfold helplessly the moment their skin touches mine. For the first time in days, I can sense light against my scrunched eyelids. I open them just a crack and am blinded. After they adjust, I see that I am being ushered toward a large archway that opens into a small arena. It is oval with rows of seats rising to the ceiling. There are many bodies in those seats, all wearing hoods that cover their faces. Black, gray, blue, and green hoods sit so still that I want to believe there is nothing alive under them.

My human instincts set off a chain reaction of alarms, telling me hundreds of sets of unseen eyes are watching me. Erratic breaths stumble between dozens of thoughts fighting to be heard in my head, but soon one emerges victorious. *RUN.* I think it with every gasp. *Run. Run. Run.*

"Tell us your name young one." An ancient voice sounds throughout the room as I'm dropped to the ground in the center of the arena. It makes the hair on my body stand straight up and silences my panicky thoughts. I cringe imagining what the being looks like, grateful it hides in shadows. Merrick said Lymerians once preyed on humans, drinking them dry. Knowing Merrick, I didn't believe him—he would never hurt a human. Now I understand that I am the prey.

Everything is still. No one moves, not even me. The rest must be here to watch me die. They will make an example out of me to teach the others not to fall in love with a human.

"Angelica Franklin," I whisper from my hunkered position.

"Do you know where you are?"

I cringe. I can't do this. Tremors start in my hands and spread through my entire body. When I look down at my shaking fingers, I see tears staining my skirt.

"ANGELICA!" it shouts into my right ear, suddenly—yet soundlessly—so close. I flinch away as the silk of its black cloak brushes my skin. *Answer.*

"Krisenica," I exhale, using every bit of my strength to push the word out. My body sobs harder.

"And who lives in Krisenica?" It no longer shouts, but its tone is condescending. I've lost all control. On my knees, I convulse and gasp for air, taking bigger breaths but getting less and less air. In my terror, a new thought repeats itself. *I didn't know, I didn't know, I didn't know.* I didn't know, didn't understand what we were up against. I hate myself for playing games with Merrick. This is not a game.

"Lymerians." I choke on the word as breath catches in my throat. Then I hear whispers, hundreds of them.

"Angelica Franklin, you are doing very well. Now, tell us, where is *Merrick*?" Loathing and evil saturate the name I love so well. I can't imagine what this thing will do once it finds Merrick. A new panic seizes me. While my suffering will soon end, the torture for Merrick will continue for decades if they catch him. I resolve that I'll die before I tell them where to find him.

My sobs stop, chest stills, hands steady.

"I don't know." My voice is flat and cold, barely audible over the growing whispers. I keep my eyes on the floor, ignoring my instinct to escape the creature circling me.

"What did you say to me?" It moves in a blur; its breath cool on my face. "You are his human. I DO NOT BELIEVE YOU!"

I stay still. The whispers close in, louder and louder until a single word silences them.

"Move."

Obediently I lift my head to look into this alien's slanted yellow eyes, my last bit of fear evaporating. The voice, bolder now, repeats the word.

"Move."

I am compelled to obey. Immediately, I thrust both of my hands at the thing in front of me and turn, pushing up, using all the strength in my limbs. It flies across the room. Merrick's blood is still strong inside me, but this is more than his blood. My brain doesn't want to think, it wants to move.

I move as one by one they converge to me, flooding the floor from the seats around the arena. I push, pull, kick, spin, but it isn't enough. They are many, and they are stronger. The whispers are gone, replaced by the sounds of bodies shifting, hitting, falling.

Sixty seconds go by, and I don't understand how I'm still fighting. Everything is on fire inside of me, yet I keep swinging at the few in the circle closest to me. The rest struggle to get to me from several feet away.

After it feels like I've been fighting a lifetime, the voice returns to save me. "Stop." It's a woman's voice. The command rings through me, instantly shutting my body down. I collapse into a heap on the floor, fully human again.

Screaming fills the arena. It goes on and on until somewhere in my muddled mind I understand that the screams are mine. Every time I move, my body roars in protest. I suppress the urge to crawl away and stop moving. Those nearest to me back away slowly. I exhale in relief at my reprieve, not caring why I am no longer the target of their attacks.

Just as I am about to give in to an exhaustion unlike anything I have ever experienced, I sense him. Ever since the first taste of his blood, I always know when he is near.

"Merrick." My heart swells with him this close, but fear overshadows the joy as I realize what it means for both of us. Then he is next to me, gently pulling me to him. Joy and agony sing in a twisted harmony as he buries his face in my hair.

"Why did you come back?" I say, crying tears of joy into his shoulder.

"I want to be human, but I could not live if I let them kill you." He kisses me, then leans his forehead against mine. "We can still be together. I can face this if you will wait for me." Anguish for all that he is losing weighs on each word.

"They won't let me leave here. Even if they do, I'll be old when they free you. You won't still love me." Sadness engulfs me as I say those final words. I clutch Merrick and kiss him again, knowing any minute the Lymerians could end my life, but they just watch silently. Why aren't they stopping us? Why isn't Merrick being taken away?

And with the power of a hundred bricks, it hits me.

"No," I gasp.

"Listen to me." Merrick looks around the room and puts his hands on either side of my face. "You cannot die because of me. Too many have died because of me." Something in his eyes changes, and he doesn't look like the boy I fell in love with. These eyes are frantic, unraveling. "I must confess, you could never outrun them. I gave you my blood in case we were caught. I had to show them you were worth keeping alive. I could not let you die, but I could not let you go either."

"I'd rather die than live as many lives as you have."

Merrick looks up in desperation, searching the room. I follow his gaze, trying to see what he seeks. His eyes finally settle, but I can't pick out who or what he's found. For several heartbeats, his eyes linger. Then his lips brush against my ear.

"I am afraid you no longer have a choice in the matter. I promise the time will pass quickly." He kisses my forehead one last time before hands rip him from me. Without Merrick to support me, my broken body slides to the ground.

The hooded creatures keep Merrick in my eyesight so that I can see as they bite and draw blood from his body. I watch, with no more tears to cry, while they prepare him for imprisonment. Red rises to Merrick's olive skin through jagged teeth marks. Over and over they shift and move, leaving no part of his skin unscathed.

I shut my eyes and think about the sister I leave behind, letting the darkness close in on me. Whether I die human or live a near eternal Lymerian life, Rebecca will be lost to me. I will not be there for her wedding day or when she welcomes her first child. Merrick's screams break into my thoughts, so I succumb to darkness. My human body must be badly broken, maybe too broken for them to save me. The world around me slowly dims—

"No!" The now familiar voice of my interrogator bellows, jolting me awake. "You will join us, Angelica. You belong here."

A wave of euphoria spreads through me. The end is near. My eyes waver, desperate to close again. "Kill him. We shall take her." The order sends a shock through my heart, igniting a desperate surge through my limbs. I launch myself at the alien. Arms wrap around me, pulling me away long before I touch its skin.

They have me. Dull pressure on my skin registers in my brain as bites. Eventually they dump me to the ground. The thread that once connected Merrick to me so fiercely flickers softly—he is very close and very weak. If only I could see him one more time, but my body will not move. This must be the end.

"Look." She is back in my thoughts, and I feel solace. My head turns to glimpse Merrick a few feet from me. At first it seems like he is looking into my eyes, but then I realize his eyes stare blankly. Like a candle flame struggling in the wind to stay lit, our connection flickers a final time and goes out. Grief swallows me, but there is soon mercy.

"Sleep."

Chapter 2

Clara

"Will the Architect come forward?" Anubis asks the silent arena. Even at this distance, I note the satisfaction written across his face. He looks less menacing now that the show is over, but that does not change what he truly is—a snake.

Anger boils deep inside me. I leave it buried. There is an art to containing such a wealth of anger and emotion while appearing docile. Two thousand years of turmoil on this planet has taught me well. It is this anger that gives me pause. I do not want this. Out of all the Lymerians, I want it least. But the human girl hears my voice and obeys my commands, binding her to me by the Laws of Liturgy. My muscles contract to propel me through the air and across the arena. When I land effortlessly on bended knee, every cloak in the room goes still.

Anubis's expression does not change. His thoughts hide behind a glossy stare and slightly parted lips. Two bloody Guards, Jordan and Kyle, appear at my side. They fought well for her, though they were no match for my Slayers. Time stands still as they all wait for me to start.

"Jordan, Kyle, we need to take her to the medic wing now." Arietta, one of my oldest confidants, is nearest to me. I nod to her. "Take him." Arietta selects two others to help her, but the rest wait. "Start with the Council." Heartbeats flutter or choke at my audacity. To my knowledge, the Council has never donated to a human transit, but I do not care about how it has always been done. This is my human, and soon she will be my Votary. Liturgy is on my side, and we do this my way.

Anubis locks his eyes with mine. I can hear the other six council members moving from their place of power toward the center of the pit where the rest of us stand.

"All others *leave.*"

The rest of the Lymerians do so quietly and swiftly. All seven elders are very close now. Jordan and Kyle remain at my side; law and duty binds them to her and me until we choose to release them. In a confrontation, they would have to fight with me as the Lymerian Laws of Liturgy supersede all others. We will not fight today, but a Vegar is always calculating the odds of survival. War can come at any time.

"Do you mean to summon Etherial as well?" Anubis wants to push the boundaries in every facet of this process. I ignore him. Anubis knows as well as I that Astros cannot participate in Liturgy. It will be years before she encounters Etherial.

I turn in the direction of the medic. Kyle lifts the girl as if he fears breaking her. It is much too late for that. This human is badly broken. Jordan stays next to me while the seven others follow. There is no time to waste with a failing human life, and within seconds we are in the medic room, crowded with Dormant doctors taking vacations from their human lives.

I stand back as the seven donate their precious blood, blood that will hopefully activate the Lymerian genetic code hidden deep inside her. Broken, beaten, and starving, her cells yearn for something to cure the hunger and heal the body. We will give her Lymerian blood. Instead of fixing her human form, it will overtake it. There is no doubt in my mind that her ancestral lineage contains someone of our kind.

She will survive this.

*   *   *

"Once she is strong enough, we will move her to the dungeons. Perhaps ten days, maybe less." Jordan is the first to speak once the seven council members leave, and the human's heart is beating strong on its own. I turn to him, wondering why he thinks the Vegar needs a lesson on Liturgy, but he is looking at Kyle.

"Thanks," Kyle mutters from across the room. Jordan turns his attention back to the hallway. Kyle, on the other hand, keeps his eyes fixed on the human. I stand and move about the room, needing to rid myself of the excess energy building inside me.

Now that the human's life is no longer in danger, I can focus on the greater issue. A Vegar Architect is unheard of. My place is with my Slayers, not a pair of Guards and a human. Why does she obey my voice? The answer hovers on the edge of my understanding, within reach but not without effort. For once, I sit still and shut my eyes in concentration.

"Clara," Jordan says softly, hours later. The sound of his voice does something to lessen the urgency of my own thoughts even though he addresses me informally. Only now do I see he thinks it will be like it was in our youth—friends and equals. No one is equal to the Vegar. There are few above and many below.

"*And nothing shall come between the three*," Kyle recites mockingly, a sly smile on his lips. Words given to us by the Astros who wrote the Laws of Liturgy hold a promise and are unbreakable. Kyle is young and can jest at these few words, but they mean something to me. "You may be the most powerful Slayer in Krisenica, Vegar, but you are stuck with us." Kyle spreads his arms wide in perfect synchronization with his growing smile. "Can I call you Clara too?"

I scoff and remind myself that I am more than just the most powerful Slayer. I am the deadliest of the Lymerians. Yet this is my new reality, a twenty-year sentence with two alarmingly different Guards when the company I crave lies within the caves—my Slayers. There is a reason the divisions keep to themselves. Guards and Slayers historically do not get along. Their essences are in competition with one another. Slayers end life and Guards protect it.

"You are also the Architect," Jordan adds, as if anyone could forget. The authority of his tone stands out in contrast to Kyle's jovial one, reassuring me that Liturgy is never wrong.

"It is real, isn't it?" Kyle asks, a sense of wonder in his voice. All three of us, even Kyle, have been alive long enough to witness transit ceremonies and see others stand where we now stand. Our lives are forever altered, fated to intertwine with each other from this day forward. I resolve to set aside my own worries and focus on the human life ending to give birth to a Lymerian one.

I walk closer to the bed and lay my hand upon human's forehead. Her body sweats as it pitifully fights to heal her. It needs more help. There is an IV line already on her lower arm, awaiting its next donor.

"I need a Dormant to move this line," I say quietly, and a female appears by my side. She is not one that I recognize. Dormants are difficult to recall by name since they spend most of their time living among humans.

"Where would you like it, Vegar?"

I stare back in judgement, enjoying the fear dance across her eyes. What kind of Lymerian sets aside their most precious gifts to live like a human?

"Where her heart beats." I point to a spot on her neck where the vein pulses in time with her overworking heart. The Dormant obeys as I sit next to the bed and hold out my arm. A moment later we are one. Immediately her heartbeat and breathing slow, the tension in her body slackens, and calm trickles through her.

"I will donate as long as I can, then one of you will take my place," I say to Kyle and Jordan. "Someone needs to go to the court and get a vial of blood from Samuel." This instruction is to the Dormants that are listening nearby. Which one of them will be brave enough to walk into the Slayer's den?

I lean back in my seat, settling in to donate for as long as possible. Eventually my eyelids start to grow heavy, my head dipping to the side.

"Switch?" Kyle is already next to me, gesturing to a Dormant. I nod, weak and vulnerable. Jordan reaches out with a small vial. I hesitate, remembering the last time I tasted another's blood—long ago. Older Lymerians like me do not need to take in blood or anything else to sustain our strength. I drink, my empty cells soaking up Samuel's warrior blood. A few drops are all it takes to restore me.

"Dormant blood will do her little good," I say, seeing her color is not much improved. "Jordan, choose five Guards. Then I will call five Slayers. Beyond that, she will suffice on what we can provide her."

"Then the dungeons," Kyle says theatrically from his place next to Angelica. Already he looks like he belongs to her. Kyle is hundreds of years old but still a young Lymerian, similar to what humans call a teenager. The moment Jordan and Kyle stepped forward, I knew Kyle would be Guard to Angelica and Jordan Guard for me. Now he gazes at her with a helplessness I have never seen him wear. I pity him. He has no choice in this, and her heart belongs to another.

"The dungeons are necessary. She will be dangerous to herself and others for many years," Jordan says, back from giving directions to the Dormants. "Particularly because Clara is Architect. *Both sire and son shall be equally balanced.*" He quotes again from the ancient scripture.

Jordan has spoken what everyone was thinking when I stepped forward, what I have been thinking since she heard my voice. How can the Vegar be the Architect? What reason warrants a Votary with strength of will equal to the deadliest of the Lymerians? There is only one answer. This Liturgy is different.

"Two remain here at all times. You each have one hour a day to coordinate your usual business. Speak to no one, not even Isaac, and especially not the Council."

Chapter 3

Clara

Our lives change now that we are a part of Liturgy. The other Lymerians instinctively put distance between themselves and us. All relationships must be on hold during Liturgy, and in some cases, may be over forever. No one that participates in Liturgy is ever the same, no matter how many centuries they live.

Kyle speaks little of the changes happening around us, content to be at her side day and night. I am aware that Kyle is no ordinary Guard. Isaac, the Guard commander, purposely assigns Kyle posts in the human world, because that is where he truly belongs. Jordan and I suspect that his demeanor has nothing to do with his natural disposition. His thoughts are only of her. He is already in love with her.

I suspect Jordan's outlook on this Liturgy is similar to mine. We are from the same surge, and in our youth, before I was named a Slayer and he a Guard, we were close. His sense of duty will mask his frustration in being chosen. Harder still, he leaves behind a mate. Years apart will not threaten their bond, but the laws attached to Liturgy will.

* * *

After seven days in the medic wing, Angelica's body is strong enough to move. Asleep, her mind is healing and coping with this alternate reality. Merrick's execution, the loss of her human life, and never being able to see her family again are but a few travesties she must endure. It is far too much for a young human mind to bear.

The pathways are empty as we move Angelica to her new home, a dungeon with the sole purpose of keeping dangerous things in. Kyle carries her while I lead, and Jordan follows behind us. As we walk silently into the depths of Krisenica, no one speaks. This part, transporting her to the cell, is the most dangerous.

It takes much longer to get through the endless tunnels than normal. We are all eager to get her there, but Kyle keeps a slow stride for her comfort. As our walk continues, my instincts begin to sense danger. Jordan and Kyle feel it too. Our heartbeats accelerate, increasing in rhythm with every passing moment.

"No one would follow us down here," Jordan offers, trying to ease our mutual tension. "There are no enemies lurking in the shadows of Krisenica. Humans cannot find her. So . . ."

"So why are we fighting the compulsion to make a break for it?" Kyle finishes Jordan's thought. "There must be a threat." He is right. Suddenly I realize what is happening and stop moving. Kyle and Jordan close the gaps between us. I turn my head to glance behind me at Angelica.

"She is becoming conscious. Move."

Jordan takes the lead, calling back any oddities in the floor or walls that might be a hazard at the speed we are now all traveling. Kyle shares the responsibility of carrying Angelica with me. Between the two of us, we have her body tightly bound in case we do not make it before she wakes.

"Here," Jordan says in just enough time for us to stop safely. All three of us work quickly to lay her long limbs gently on the floor. My heart is hammering, threatening to explode. Before I can force it back to calm I realize it is not my heart. It is hers. With the few seconds I have left, I scan every inch of the cell, then fall back with Jordan and Kyle. Unnecessarily, all three of us rock back to secure the door in place. Kyle turns the handle, and the lock creaks into place. A moment later, she screams. Jordan and I grab Kyle and run full speed back the way we came.

Our quarters are a long way from Angelica's room but still far below the rest of Krisenica. There are four identical rooms, two on either side of the hallway, and none have doors. We stand before the rooms and stare into them until Kyle breaks the silence.

"A bit of a letdown I suppose, but it will do." He sighs and chooses a room. "You'd think the Astros could see this coming," Kyle continues to joke halfheartedly as he unpacks the few things he brought with him, including vials of blood. Jordan takes the room next to Kyle, leaving one for me and one to wait for Angelica.

"Everything they say about the Astros is true," I announce, needing to defend them even though I realize Kyle is simply making light of our circumstance.

"What makes you so sure?" Kyle asks. "There are many tales about the Astros, they can't all be true.

"She is the Vegar, Kyle, a commander." A hint of pride slips into Jordan's words. Even after centuries apart, my victories are his.

I stay quiet as I choose a room, refusing to let even one memory sneak out of its cage. Kyle is taciturn as well; Jordan's explanation satisfies him.

Within the security of these walls I exhale. It seems like I have been holding my breath for a week. Up there, I will always be Vegar. Down here, in our solitude, I can just be Angelica's Architect. Somewhere between the medic wing and the dungeons, I shed my Vegar skin. My instinctive need to be with my Slayers shifts its focus to her. I need to be with her, near her. The Astros are never wrong and neither is Liturgy.

* * *

For the next three months, we observe. There is a small room close to the elevator that allows us to watch her. It has several monitors that connect to cameras within the cell and hallway. We can record sound and image reviewable only from this room. One of us is always watching her. We use what we see to determine our path forward. Jordan and Kyle weigh in with their ideas, but my decisions are final. Eventually, I will make first contact.

After a few hours of screams, Angelica gives up, falling into an immobile lump on the floor. Even now, she sits as she did nearly ninety days ago. Inevitably, her body withers. Once beautiful blonde hair is now white to match her pale skin. Blue veins show through her skin as her body weakens without blood.

Jordan is impassive toward her deteriorating state, but Kyle grows darker with every passing day. At first, he continues to jest, upholding his well-known sarcasm, but then he shifts. Smiles turn into empty stares and then open scowls. I am not surprised that Kyle struggles to control his emotions. He is young and loves her. As a Guard, he is used to making critical decisions on his own and likely finds this kind of collaboration difficult. Just as I, the Vegar, leader of the Slayers, am not used to heeding the council of others. Until we trust each other, someone must bend. My tolerance for Kyle's youth is running thin.

"When, Clara? She is wasting away." Kyle paces in the viewing room, eyes shifting to the screens every few seconds trying to stare life back into her.

"This is the process Kyle." I reply exactly the same way as I always do. Kyle does not respond; instead, he goes very quiet and still. Though we are part of Liturgy together and I should be able to trust him, my gut tells me he is about to become unhinged. This time when I speak, I make sure there is an edge to my tone. "I will go when I am ready."

I turn back to my screen, settling into my chair for the long shift. Kyle is no match against me; perhaps he has gone a little mad. I hear the legs of his chair scrape against the stone floor as he shoves it aside.

"I am not a Slayer in your army, Vegar Clara. I am her Guard!" he shouts down from behind me. Kyle's massive frame towers over me, fueling his ambitions. It is not the first time my small size has given a challenger a false sense of superiority.

"There is a reason there are two Guards and one Architect." Kyle's harsh words have drawn Jordan from his room down the hall, and he now stands blocking the doorway in front of me. Everything inside of me goes calm. *So be it.*

A Guard is incredibly strong while a Slayer is unimaginably fast and viciously deadly. The strength of a Guard depends on the importance of his ward. Kyle will be stronger than the average Guard because Angelica's place as a Votary is of great importance. He also cares deeply for her, and that will afford him even greater strength. All of which mean nothing, because Angelica is not in danger, and he knows it. Wanting to give your ward comfort is not the same as saving their life.

In Kyle's defense, there have been times when Guard defeated Slayer, but the Slayer was always outnumbered. Kyle is counting on Jordan's presence and their recent increase in strength to even the odds with me. There is just one problem.

In an instant, the chair beneath me becomes my weapon. The heavy steel will land blinding blows in my hands. When fighting a Guard, you must not stop until they are unconscious. Their physical strength will overpower anyone they can get their hands on. Therefore, I must keep landing hits until his body gives up.

After the first three hits, Kyle loses his balance. I toss the chair aside and go for his throat. For many Slayers, it would be a mistake, but I have a point to make and am not afraid of his strength.

His height advantage makes him impossible for me to lift, so I take him to the ground. My hand squeezes around his throat as I lean into him, pinning his legs with my feet and forcing his head to the left side. My other hand digs into one of his arms, leaving the other free, daring him to use it. Kyle's eyes glance to Jordan, who is still standing in the doorway.

"Have you heard the rumors? Blink once for yes and twice for no." One blink. "It is all true. Which is why you are incapacitated and still conscious. I am letting just enough air escape into your lungs so that you will not sleep. It is very uncomfortable I imagine." Jordan exhales from above us. "I am the goddamn *Vegar*!" I shout at him as my anger reaches its peak. "That means I have beaten every other Slayer that exists in this world, including my predecessor. And Angelica is *my* Votary! She will be equally matched to *me*. Can you imagine what could happen if I cannot control her? If none can stop her? Did you see her strength when she was still human?"

One blink.

"Clara," Jordan says, and I let go of Kyle's throat instantly. I retrieve my chair and sit back down at the monitor.

Kyle takes deep breaths. Once his breathing steadies, he looks accusingly at Jordan, wondering how I won him over. Guards do not side with Slayers, especially against their own. Clearly, Kyle does not remember all the Laws of Liturgy.

Jordan sighs. "Do not look at me like that, Kyle. You said it yourself, for God sakes. There are two Guards and one Architect for a reason. One Guard for the Votary and one Guard for the Architect. Even if I did agree with you, I could not side against her."

Kyle says nothing, only glares his bloodshot eyes at Jordan.

"Tomorrow," I say, breaking the tension in the room. Kyle's attack reminds me exactly what I am capable of. My triumph over him was nearly effortless. While the Astros promise a Votary to match their Architect, it will not be for many years. When Angelica reaches her full potential as a Lymerian, her strength of will shall equal mine. In the meantime, I can control her in other ways if it comes to that. My voice in her head during Liturgy proves she will listen to me, but I am not sure how long that connection will last.

The next day we silently walk the narrow path to the deepest part of the dungeons. Once the pathway narrows and the air starts to stale, I know we are close. "Stop." My command is a whisper, but both abruptly halt. In the beginning, her contact and trust must start with me. Here their presence will go unnoticed, though they remain close enough to help if something goes wrong.

Slowly I walk forward. A few more steps and the girl may be able to hear my boots hit the ground, the beating of my heart, and air filling my lungs and spilling out. All of her senses will need training for her to control the stimuli, to keep from getting overwhelmed. I walk cautiously—even steady steps and breaths—until I catch the faintest scent of blood.

"Angelica," I breathe. It takes me several more minutes of measured steps to reach her door. She is not moving, not so much as a breath since I spoke her name. Slowly, I reach my hand out to the handle.

Angelica must realize the door is about to open because she finally stirs. The movement is quick and quiet but deliberate. My lips curl slightly into a grin and the weight inside me eases. She is preparing to fight, something I do better than anyone. To think I wasted weeks worrying about our first encounter. Without any further hesitation, I slide the lock and open the door.

The instant my hand slips off the door handle, it swoops around and finds her neck. With ease, I thrust Angelica to the far side of her cell. I place myself in the frame of the door. Angelica continues, attack after attack. Each one is sloppy, untrained, and commanded by a brain in shock. Though she is powerful and fast, I am faster and stronger. There will be no need to use our connection to stop her.

Minutes tick by without her body showing signs of exhaustion. Regretfully, I know I will have to put her down. This time, as I block each hit, I break a finger until all of them are bent and gnarled. Angelica keeps attacking, able to ignore the discomfort in her hands.

Suddenly, I think about Kyle listening in the hallway. They are close enough to hear what is happening. It is likely very upsetting for him. I brush away the thought, knowing his emotions cannot affect my course for Angelica. Time to be the Architect.

I snap her back. She crumbles into a heap on the ground, letting a faint cry escape her lips. Now that she is debilitated, it is safe to abandon my position at the door. I kneel beside her. Angelica is a fitting name as she embodies what humans call an angel. She does not look as she did when I last viewed her. The fight has brought life to her.

Thick strands of newly whitened hair glitters, much like the way ice glistens under the moonlight. Stunning pale blue eyes glare waves of anger at me. Her skin is perfectly smooth and robust. Angelica is absolutely breathtaking.

"Angelica, age seventeen. The year is 1958. This is the ninety-fourth day of your isolation and the first attempt to allow you contact. My name is Vegar Clara. You have failed this examination. Your next contact will be in three hundred and sixty-five days." I ease myself up and walk backward slowly, my eyes locking with hers. It is a terrifying site. Angelica's broken hands are on the ground, palms supporting her. Despite her suffering, she manages to position herself on all fours. Her broken back sinks toward the ground. Though her stare chills me, I keep my gaze deadly.

Once I have the massive door shut, I rest against it for two breaths then push myself away toward the dreary dungeon hall. Kyle and Jordan are waiting where I left them. Both look exactly as they did minutes ago, which means Kyle did not try to fight.

As I near, I notice both of them staring at me with matching curious—even fearful? — looks. When I move to walk by them, Jordan's hand brushes against my check. On his thumb, the tiniest smear of blood.

Now the look on their faces make sense. My Votary made a mark on me, bled *me.* Ordinarily this would spark a multitude of emotions—anger, shock, irritation. Instead, I fill with sweet anticipation for what is to come. Everything we were told of the ceremony and Liturgy has proven true so far, this final piece being the most important.

I am the only one here strong enough to survive being her Architect.

Chapter 4

Angelica

"Good is good." Soft words lull me from the abyss that lingers between dreams and reality. At first, I see a foggy mixture of light and shadow as I fight to gain my bearings in this lucid place. Everything feels very familiar, even that voice. All at once my senses sharpen, and I whirl to face to the child staring up at me.

Rebecca looks younger than the last time I saw her, sitting primly next to me in her favorite red sweater—the one she wore the first time we met. It's not just the childish sweater that dates her, but the hair style as well. Rebecca's dirty blonde hair is cut just above the shoulders, not flowing midway down her back as I remember. This can't be.

Déjà vu ripples through me as I stare into Rebecca's childish face. I remember this. It's the day I met Rebecca at the orphanage, residence of my haunted childhood. I must be dreaming. *Wake up!* I think to myself. *Wake up, right now*. What's the last real thing that happened? Where am I? *Wake up!*

Suddenly I smell stale, cool air, and know I'm still in their dungeon. I lose the scent and float back in the dream. *Harder*, I think. *Try harder to wake.* This time I manage to force my eyes open for real, but I can't see anything. Frantically I blink over and over, but it's no use. I'm sitting on the bed with Rebecca again. I give up trying to see reality.

The room comes to life. Rows of beds appear with gray, wooly blankets tucked neatly around them, orphans lounging on top. Windows line the tall white walls framing a world that has forgotten about us. I look back toward Rebecca and my heart hurts. Maybe this is real? All I want is to reach out to her, to hug her and smell her hair.

"It's real and it's not real." I startle at Rebecca's soft, high voice. Here, as so often in real life, she guesses exactly what I'm thinking. Dream be damned. I pull her to me, realizing this is the closest I will ever get to seeing her again.

"I've ruined everything," I whisper in her ear. "I have no idea where I am or what they plan to do with me. They've drugged me somehow and no matter how hard I try, I can't wake up." We pull apart, and I notice Rebecca's eyes look greener than usual—nearly glowing.

"You're not ready to wake up, Angelica." For so long I saw her as a child that needed me to protect her, but in this dream, she is the one with all the answers. "Janice is here. You should go talk to her." As soon as Rebecca says those words, my feet take me across the room without my permission. Janice's tiny body is folded on her bed, bent over drawing papers. Her short black hair is pulled back in a greasy ponytail, face set in a permanent scowl.

Before I reach her, I reconsider, forcing my feet still. This isn't how it really happened. The day I met Rebecca, we talked on my bed—purposely ignoring Janice. Rebecca promised her family would adopt me, but I couldn't bring myself to tell Janice until my last night at the orphanage. I always regretted not telling her sooner. Janice is the only friend I've ever earned on my own. Our friendship wasn't arranged or made legal by signing papers but born in mutual despair within these walls. Maybe this is my chance to make it right.

"A family wants to adopt me," I say when I'm close enough for only Janice to hear. I did want her opinion that day, yet at the same time I was scared she'd give a hundred reasons not to go. Janice doesn't look up. Her eyes keep steady on what she is creating with pencil and paper, nurturing her one talent. Moments pass and she still won't look at me. I turn to leave.

"I nearly told you it wasn't gonna end well." My heart tears at the sound of Janice's slow, soft drone. It is the sound of abandonment, a child losing the last thing she has to love. I want to wrap my arms around her, declare that I love her and always will. But my words will never reach Janice's ears, because this isn't real. When I move back to face her, she's still working on her drawing.

"It wouldn't have made a difference. You did the right thing, Janice," I tell her. Janice will carry the heaviest burden of guilt from my disappearance. I close my eyes, fighting off the tears. I hate myself for leaving her that day and for every argument that passed between us this year. If I had stayed in the orphanage, it could have saved us both. Janice's eyes finally leave the paper, and they are lit with an anger I know all too well.

"I won't make it without you. When I wanted to quit this life, you were here to give me somethin' to live for. You said we'd get outta this place someday. Now you're leavin' me here alone." Janice looks back down, and her pencil starts moving again.

"I'm sorry," I say and take her hand, pulling it away from the paper.

"Now you're gone forever." This, out of everything, stings the most. Unless my corpse is found, Janice will search for me until her dying breath. She will die disappointed. Worse, she is the only one that knew I was leaving with Merrick. Janice will relive the dread of that night, punishing herself for not stopping me.

A sound from far off catches my attention and sends prickles down my spine. I glance around the room, but it's empty again. When I look back at Janice, she's gone. A slight breeze touches my face, carrying a familiar smell. *Merrick.*

My eyes snap open, and this time I can clearly see the dungeon walls around me. I'm still here. How long has it been? Boots click against stone in the distance, slowly getting louder. Wild, incoherent images flash in my mind as I try to listen. So much blood. The faint wisp of Merrick's smell is real and drawing nearer, but there are other smells as well. It's not Merrick coming to rescue me. Someone else is coming, but they were with Merrick recently.

They're at the door. I move without understanding why; there isn't anywhere to hide. My brain explodes with a hundred thoughts at once. *Danger, Merrick, run, fight, scream, it's a woman, make her take you to Merrick.* I attack. Then she is above me, and my body is broken.

The sound of her voice triggers every memory I have of Krisenica. Three days in a dungeon, two men walking me to my death, the arena, the alien, fighting, screaming, pain, *move,* Merrick, *sleep.* Merrick is dead. How simple for the Lymerians to replace one of their own with some human like me. His life, the many lifetimes he lived, was worth so much more than that death.

My body starts to vibrate with the need to take action, but it's broken. With all my strength, I manage to lift myself on all fours and stare at her. She is one of them, but the same as Merrick, humanlike. Her onyx eyes lock on mine, and in them I can see that she is not my enemy. The door shuts, and I let myself drop back down.

If she is not my enemy, then why am I broken? Why does she smell like Merrick? What's a Vegar? I crumble—back and fingers howling for attention. *Sleep*, my body begs.

I fight the temptation to shut my eyes. Instead I try to decipher the jumbled thoughts bouncing around in my mind. They are moving too fast, changing direction from one second to the next. It is not long before I succumb to my body's wishes and sleep.

Chapter 5

Clara

Hours have gone by in silence since I crippled Angelica. Every few minutes, there is a squeak as someone swivels their chair to glance back at the unchanging picture. We are spread throughout the small viewing room in varying shades of contemplation. Jordan is reflective while I pulse with the need to forge our path forward. Kyle is sulking because Angelica is sleeping again. Bickering over when to go in has done us no good. I can take the silence no longer.

"There are three of us, which means three different perspectives," I announce, looking from Jordan to Kyle. They both stay still as stone, so I continue with my own assessment. "Her transition is complete: she is no longer a human." Kyle exhales and his heartbeat pauses for a few seconds. Jordan jerks his head at me, but Kyle's heart is beyond either of us and always will be.

"How do you know?" Kyle's voice comes out hoarse, barely above a whisper. His newly reddened eyes are still set on the unmoving Angelica. There is a part of me that accepts Kyle cannot help his love for her, but the Vegar in me refuses to submit to his incessant questioning. He cannot possibly think I am in error. I broke her back—a risk I would not have taken with a human body.

"I was in the same room as her," I snap. Jordan's face is stern as he catches my eye, extinguishing my threatening flame. When I look at Kyle again, his head is resting between shaky palms. I pause and begin again in a more even tone. "Human eyes could not see in that room. She heard my steps long before human ears could. Not only were her attacks strong, they were precise, if untrained." Kyle looks up in time to see my finger trace the edge of my cheek.

"What else?" Jordan asks, sensing I am holding back.

"These cameras are poor quality." I nod to the black and white screens. "You cannot tell, but she no longer looks like a human nor Dormant, or like any of our kind born on Earth."

"Because the Council gave her blood?" Kyle asks.

"I am not sure," I answer honestly. "Blood is meant to activate the transition. One dose of blood can temporarily alter the physical appearance of our kind. This appears to be permanent. We will know more in time. But . . ."

"It is unlikely her appearance will differ with time," Jordan finishes for me.

"So she's . . ." Kyle trails off. In unison, the three of us slowly turn back to the monitors.

"*She has skin without color, eyes as clear as the sea, and hair that glistens like snow*." Jordan recites the words of the scriptures about the first Lymerians to come to Earth. Lymeria, our home planet, is mostly ice and brutally cold. Lymerian bodies were once a reflection of that environment. His guess is correct.

I nod. "She is how our kind looked before they began to feed on humans." It has been thousands of years since the Lymerians fed from human blood, but it forever changed their physical appearance. The only reason they ceased drinking blood was because it made them weaker.

"Then we agree her transition is complete. Now, tell us why you broke her back so quickly."

"And why we're leaving her alone for a year." Kyle's tone is no longer weak. It is bitter, teetering on hostile. Once again, his emotions are getting away from him.

I turn to face him, my look long and hard, before answering either one of them. "Physically her transition is complete, but her mind needs time to catch up. It is not ready—would not let her stop attacking me."

"Why for a year?" Kyle asks, his voice somewhat calmer now.

"If I return too soon, the outcome will be the same. A year is the longest I am willing to leave her without feeding. Let us hope that is enough time."

Kyle scoffs at my answer. His eyes scream with disagreement and defiance. There will be time to dwell on that later. It is their turn to speak.

"Now tell me about the hallway. How did you keep Kyle from coming into the cell?" Both of them gaze at me, the same hollow expression on their faces. It launches me into action.

I move to the monitors and play back the footage from the hallway during that time period. We walk as three until I raise my hand, and everyone stops. My figure leaves the frame, and they stand frozen in their places. Both men stand straight with their arms down at their sides. They do not move the entire time I am with Angelica. It is not until they see my figure again that their bodies relax.

"You could not move? Neither of you?" My eyes lock with Jordan's. Perhaps Kyle's current demeanor has less to do with Angelica's predicament and more to do with his own. When I do not shift my gaze, Jordan's brow furrows in concern. At least he does not resent me. I rise, clearing my head with every measured click of my heels.

There are whispers that Architects can commune with their Votaries in many ways and command them if they so choose. The Ceremony calls upon this connection in order to identify the Architect, but thereafter only upon necessary circumstances should it be used.

Why would an Architect need to control a Guard for Liturgy? The answer comes as suddenly as I have the thought. Not all Architects are Slayers, and none ever Vegar. A Guard could over power many Lymerians, especially Litmars and Dormants. They would have to overpower the Architect's Guard, but Kyle's passion from yesterday shows it can be done.

I blink and tear my eyes away from Jordan. A new sensation fills me, one that rarely makes appearances for a Vegar. Relief. Knowing that I am completely in control allows me to drop the wall that constantly divides me from everyone else. For centuries, I have worn it as armor so that I will be feared, followed, and obeyed.

My room and bed beckon me, promising a night of deep, restful sleep. Just as I am about to drift off, I hear a soft rustle as Jordan settles in to the chair next to my bed. A reprimand dies before it can escape my lips. Somewhere inside of me lives a small piece that wants him to stay.

* * *

While Angelica serves a year in solitude, spoken words between our trio become fewer until there are none at all. The problem lies in Angelica. She is the common thread that ties us together and while she sleeps, we lose our purpose. Early on, we develop individual shifts, taking turns watching the monitors for movement or change. There is none. Until my one-year deadline, there is no point in discussing anything.

Like the true Lymerians we are, our bodies adapt to our surroundings. Without words, our other senses tune in to each other. Soon, I do not need Kyle to tell me that he enjoys watching Angelica sleep because I can feel it. When he sits down for his shift and sees Angelica on the screen, his happiness brushes against me. Jordan's emotions are calmer than Kyle's, but they do change. His relief comes while I am watching Angelica.

Fear sows inside me with our growing transparency. As Vegar, I bury my emotions as deep as possible. No one can suspect that my heart loves and hides pain. Upstairs it is easy for me to conceal these things, but down here everything is different. If I can experience Jordan's and Kyle's deepest emotions, they can feel mine. Secrets will die before their first breath, and trust is no longer a choice. Will Kyle honor Liturgy and my secrets for the rest of his days? It is in this year of silence that Liturgy truly settles upon me. More than ever, I believe in it.

We never leave the dungeons. Jordan and I require nothing to survive, not even blood. Our bodies are old enough to regenerate cells on their own. So perfect is our ability to regenerate that we do not bathe nor concern ourselves with hygiene. Those are human rituals. Our few sets of clothing will last years. Kyle brought plenty of blood vials, anticipating he would not leave until she does. Still young, he should not go more than a few months without feeding.

During my shifts with Angelica, I wonder what she is dreaming about. Deep sleep is common to those transitioning so their minds will emerge superior and controlled. I marvel at the ingenuity. How does it work? What does she learn while she sleeps?

Her back and fingers heal fast, taking up most of the transfused blood. Because of this, starvation begins sooner than we expect. Before long, her body withers, worsening each day. By the end of the year, she is a corpse.

Days before the one-year deadline, I walk into the viewing room. It is my turn to monitor Angelica after Kyle. Instead of leaving, Kyle stays. He wants to talk. Before he can say anything, Jordan appears in the doorway. Kyle tenses and breathes heavily in irritation, but my spirits rise as we become three again.

"What's your plan, Clara?" Kyle's words do not sound like his own. This year has taken a toll on him. Gone is his easy smile and soft gaze. Instead, his lips are drawn tight and eyes sunken in. He has barely slept in weeks. I am responsible but will not let guilt touch me.

"My approach shall be identical to the first meeting," I explain. "Patterns are important for her in the beginning." I pause, wondering if I should continue or if it will only make Kyle more upset.

"What else?" Jordan prompts.

"If I could just—"

"We are not human," I begin, cutting Kyle off. "From what she has seen, we are all monsters. Monsters that can move faster than any human, hear her heart beating from across the room and kill their own for trying to run away. And we have stolen her life, her humanity.

She will fear you Kyle. We have no idea what kind of Lymerian she is and that could mean all the difference."

"I will take no part in her transition then?" Kyle asks quietly.

"I am telling you that before you take part in her transition, Angelica must believe beyond any shadow of a doubt that she can trust me. And I must trust her. It will take years."

"You know who I will be to her. The Astros decree it so." Kyle's intentions toward Angelica are obvious, but this is the first time he dares to speak aloud of prophecy.

"The prophecy decrees that the Guards shall bear love for their wards during Liturgy. It does not mean she will see you that way. She does not have to return your feelings." Kyle does not hear my words. He trusts what is in his heart and blindly believes she will experience it too. I try again to explain. "You may be fated, but consider what she tried to do to me. I am her Architect, yet that means nothing to her right now."

Kyle stalks past Jordan and out of the viewing room. I shift to Jordan, hoping to see understanding in his eyes, but they are distant. The prophecy of Guards applies to him as well, though he knows I will not speak of it in regard to the two of us. He pivots, taking crisp, even steps away from me. I deflate.

Chapter 6

Angelica

When my eyes open again, the light is blinding. I blink until the whiteness calms, allowing the rest of the room to take shape. Above me paint chips between familiar cracks that snake across the ceiling. Once I was bedridden for weeks with only strength enough to stare at these intricate patterns. This infirmary is where I was born and where I met my truest friend.

It wasn't where I was actually born, but it's the first place I remember. In 1945 the sisters of St. Mary's Catholic Orphanage took me in. I was four. When I searched for memories of before, I only saw darkness. The sisters could keep secrets better than orphans, hushing my questions and ushering me into permanent shyness.

Memories, my mind whispers, unleashing a thousand of them upon me. Each one is clear and precise in detail. They play one after another like on a reel viewer, moving forward in time until my final memory. Merrick's empty eyes. I shake the image away and search for one that fits this place.

I blink and the infirmary changes slightly to form a well taken care of memory. May 24, 1949—the day I met Janice.

"If we hadn't been sick together, hadn't spent weeks stuck next to each other in here, we never woulda been friends." Nine-year-old Janice sits in the bed next to me. Her tone is cold but familiar, and I rejoice in being with some version of her. I think about what she says and hope that it isn't true. Janice's story is sad and in the end, I fail her too.

Janice arrived at the orphanage not long before this, only a year older than me. Within a week, the other girls were terrified of her. After several weeks, the sisters kept their distance as well. It wasn't that she caused trouble or disrupted lessons. In fact, she rarely spoke. But her presence filled the room. We were always aware of her though she seemed to take no notice of us. She was a feeling that crept up the back of your neck and made your skin shiver.

I welcomed the shiver.

Janice was a change in this sad, gray place. She didn't feel off to me; everyone else felt like ghosts. Janice buzzed with a darkness that never let me forget she was there. For some reason, she liked me too.

"You're wrong, Janice."

The right side of my face goes cold and when I turn to see why, it hits glass. Quickly I turn back to Janice, but it's too late. The scenery is different. I'm in my room at the Franklin house, sitting in the bay window that overlooks the street. Most of the view is taken up by a massive tree—my tree. It's raining. The memory won't come to me, even with the rain outside to guide me. Suddenly I notice something in my hands. I smile when I see that it's my favorite book. I must have read it a dozen times. It's resting on my legs, open to page thirty-nine, waiting for me read it in my head.

> *Kitty did not know that the man in the bakery was not a new acquaintance, but in fact, an old friend. Now reader you may wonder how is it possible that Kitty did not recognize a man that she had once known so well. Our eyes are not trained to see the impossible and this was impossible.*

I stop reading and let the words sink in, but it doesn't do any good. There isn't anyone else in the room, but maybe someone is coming. Maybe I'm just supposed to sit here and wait. The window creaks its old familiar tune as my tree scratches against the glass.

I remember my owl, the one that lives in the tree. Could he be waiting for me? Does my little friend have a message? My heart starts to thunder in my chest at the idea. I squint, trying to see through the rain, but it's too dark. I reach for the latch to open the window but stop short. I'm not alone anymore.

Joy explodes through me as I realize that it's Vic, Rebecca's brother, in the room with me. My beloved book drops from my lap as I cross the room to reach him. We embrace and I relax under his touch. His arms hold tight, assuring me he won't let me disappear into another memory.

The reel clicks and a hundred cherished memories play for me. Long walks with Rebecca skipping ahead of us. Late nights playing games while the others sleep. Showing up at a school social just to make sure I didn't have to stand alone. Falling asleep together every time it thundered because I hate storms.

But what memory is this?

"Vic," I whisper in his ear. I pull back a little and am struck by the depth in his almond brown eyes. It's as if I am seeing them for the first time. His hair is buzzed even shorter than usual, and we are nearly the same height—a recent memory. "I don't remember this."

"Yes, you do. Try harder," Vic says encouragingly. Each detail of the memory turns in my head until I have it. The rain, the book, the noise at the window.

"The night before I left," I say. I had been reading by the window when it creaked. Janice's signal—she had gotten my message. Everything was exactly the same except for one thing. When I reached for the latch to the window that night, Vic hadn't been there to stop me from going down.

Slowly I pull myself back from Vic, the spell broken. "I have to go out the window. Janice is waiting for me." His grip tenses.

"I could have gotten you to stay." His pained eyes stare into mine. "If I had been home that night, you would have stayed." My breath catches. This isn't Vic's fault, it's mine. I left with Merrick and no one could have stopped me. Some part of me must believe Vic because it's in my head. These are my words even if Vic is saying them.

I drop his hands, walk to the window and jump. No reason to waste time climbing down safely in a dream. None of this is real and any moment I might wake up. I'm not ready to wake up in prison, out of control and with Merrick still dead.

My feet hit the ground, but I'm not outside my home. It's warm and the grass beneath my feet is cool and dry. *No.* Anything but a Merrick memory.

"Angelica." My blood turns to ice at the sound of Merrick's easy voice behind me. Immediately my eyes well with tears. I'm paralyzed as every moment I spent with Merrick repeats through me. The night we met at the diner is the first memory, then every other moment from the next year flashes until his final hour. One full of terror and regret.

"What are you doing here?" I choke out the words, pushing the image of his empty eyes out of my mind. Then his hand is on my shoulder, waiting for me to fall into his arms. I can't because it isn't real. He isn't real. The world spins as the reality of losing him brings me to my knees. Anger overtakes sorrow as I remember I'm in a dungeon cell in the depths of Krisenica, waiting to wake up as one of them. I *don't* want to be one of them.

"Why did you have to like me!?" I shout into the air, not having the guts to turn around and yell it to his face. On all fours, I watch as unending tears flow to the grass beneath me.

"Look at me," he says in his *time to calm down, Angelica* voice. Firm but gentle, quiet yet direct. And just like all the other times, I melt at his words. This is all my fault. He is dead because of me. I sit up and say the only thing I can before it's too late.

"I'm so sorry."

Merrick is as beautiful and youthful as the day I met him. His black hair rebelliously frames a pale face and striking green eyes. He puts his hands in his pockets and shifts his weight a little. Then he comes close and bends down, taking my face in his hands.

"Wake up." Merrick's mouth moves, but the voice isn't his. It is unmistakably *her* voice. Then just like any other dream, one moment I am in it and the next I open my eyes, awake.

This time when I open my eyes, I know.

The first time I woke up, it was to the sound of footsteps, and I thought I was in danger. Grief, anger, and confusion fueled my clumsy, silly attacks toward one of them—Vegar Clara, as she calls herself.

The first time I woke up, I couldn't think straight. This time is different. My mind is clear and my own. My senses are overflowing, taking in the surroundings. Thoughts are moving on top of each other but in perfect harmony.

Vegar Clara's right hand lifts up my chin so that I'm staring straight into her eyes. Cold, black orbs fill most of my vision, but what I do see, I see perfectly. I could count each of her eyelashes if I wanted to or the tiny creases throughout her face that tell me her age in human years. Though the air is breathable and the room brighter, it is the same room from my first days here. On the edge of my vision, I see an open door.

Every inch of my body stings—*don't move*. My life is not in danger, and even if it was, I can't escape her. I can feel each one of my cells shrinking further and further into themselves, trying desperately not to use more energy than necessary. None of my bones are broken, my fingers and back already healed.

This is starvation. I am starving.

Clara releases her grip on my chin and walks to the other side of the cell. Walks isn't the right word, really, to describe how a Lymerian moves. She takes longer strides, stronger steps, than a mere walk. The effect is graceful and quick movement. Why can a Lymerian move so much better than a human? Doesn't gravity have the same pull on them as it does on us? And, I cringe, it's not *us* anymore. I am one of them.

A sound comes from Clara's direction, and my head snaps up to her. My mind automatically relays everything about her appearance. She is small—for a human and probably for a Lymerian—yet I'd seen just how strong and fast she could be. Clara, except for face and hands, is a blot of ink, her body clothed in black to match her black hair and coal eyes. Coal eyes focused on me.

"Why are you not fighting this time?"

Her voice is bold and strong, her accent unrecognizable. She's from somewhere else.

"Because I know," I reply in a raspy voice.

"You know what?"

Before I answer, I let my new eyes sweep over her. Straight spine, set gaze, and a relaxed expression tell me she already has my answer in her head. She wants me to admit this out loud.

"I am a Lymerian now."

Clara produces a clear vial from her pocket and holds it up. Inside there is a deep red liquid. She pops the top off for just a second, then caps it. Two forces inside me work against each other as the smell invades my senses. Starvation commands my body to move *now*, to get blood. My mind reminds me that my last mistake cost me a year without feeding. Brain overpowers body.

Clara walks towards me, slow, like a human. She holds out the vial to me. "My blood."

Very gently I lift my aching fingers to the vial. Without another moment of drama or suspense, she lets me have it.

While my brain overpowered the instinct to fight for blood, I can't refuse blood readily given. The small part of me that knows her blood will change me, make me more like her, especially since my body is so weak, barely puts up a fight. This is the moment, the choice. By taking the blood, I accept what I am. I'm Lymerian, and I want blood.

I tilt my head to the ceiling and drop the entire vial into my mouth, lacking the strength to remove the stopper. The glass crunches, little pinches against my tongue and throat. My body absorbs the blood and glass quickly, quieting the stinging pains. The rubber top doesn't settle as well and a moment later, it's back in my mouth. I spit it into my hand.

"I will be back in thirty days with another vial." Clara walks slowly to the door, another test to see if I'll flee now that I'm stronger with blood. Instinct tells me Clara is much more lethal than even our first encounter proved. If she were not so strong, would I try to run? I don't move a muscle. The massive door thunders to a close.

The blood replenishes and rejuvenates me. I am brand new and near invincible. How many times did I watch Merrick perform feats of superhuman ability? Now I could do those things if I wanted to, but I won't. Thirty days. I have to make this blood last inside of me. Maybe that's an excuse. Maybe I just can't bring myself to enjoy being something I hate. I hate them for what they did to Merrick and what they are doing to me—don't I? This new body is paying attention to everything, and hating the Lymerians is nowhere near the priority it should be. The hate is fading, minute by minute, since the moment I opened my eyes.

Chapter 7

Clara

Kyle and Jordan are fixated on the cameras when I return to the viewing room. Without a word, I pull in behind them, just as curious. She is in a different part of the cell, sitting with her back against the wall, eyes shut.

"Any other movement?"

Kyle and Jordan shake their heads.

For the next fifteen minutes, I detail everything that happened while I was in the cell, especially the things they could not have seen on screen. They listen quietly, making mental notes to circle back to one part of the story or another.

"She didn't even sense you coming this time," Kyle accuses as soon as I finish.

"You are a Guard, you have witnessed the *sove* before," Jordan counters. When a Lymerian's body is starving, it goes into a deep sove, or sleep. Only the most essential body functions continue to operate. Hearing is not essential to staying alive.

"How much did the blood help?" Kyle asks, then mutters, "You didn't give her enough. She went right back to sleep." Jordan sighs and stands up to pace. Kyle pushes back on his chair, slamming himself against the wall, a childish gesture in response to my decision about the blood. We argued about the amount for hours before I left, Kyle in complete polarity with my thoughts.

"Shall I explain *again*? I would rather give her too little than too much. Perhaps she is sleeping because she wants to," I challenge.

"Or she's still in pain," Kyle returns, furious. We snap, movements mirroring as we rise from our chairs and charge at the same time, but Jordan's pacing has put him between us.

"Not again," he says, throwing out his arms. Jordan is so fast that he catches us both off guard and propels us in opposite directions. I turn with the push, flipping upside down, and I am on my feet again in time to see Kyle collide with the wall.

"You cannot seem to learn your lesson," I snarl at Kyle from my crouched position.

"And you are not acting like a leader," Jordan barks back at me.

Immediately I straighten and shift my stare to Jordan.

"You are itching for a fight, Clara, but it is not going to be with either one of us." Jordan drops his hands. "You need a trip upstairs. We all do." A part of me wants to argue with him, and if we were around anyone other than Kyle, I would.

I am different down here, beneath Krisenica . . . with *them*. I do not have to be Vegar when I am in these cells. Kyle and I rarely agree about how to proceed with Angelica, but I trust him and Jordan more than I ever thought possible. If real danger were near us, nothing would come between us. Perhaps Jordan is right.

"Fine," I say. "I will go up soon." I turn to leave.

"I am going up with you," Jordan replies before I can reach the door. I almost refuse, unwilling to leave Kyle alone with Angelica. Then I remember the power Liturgy has given me, though I am loath to use it. If Kyle were Slayer, this would be simple. Slayers operate in military fashion. They follow orders. Fights often break out within ranks, but never between them. Guards are so different.

Kyle is a Guard, and that is his highest order. If Angelica is in danger, will he act even if I forbid him from doing so? If there is not a threat, will he leave her be? Can he contain his desire to be near her?

Jordan interrupts my musings. "Clara, it is only a few hours. We should go now." I look from Kyle to the screen again. Suddenly, a strange urge to appease Jordan outweighs my reservations.

"Let her sleep," I order, and Kyle's hurt eyes find mine. For all our disagreeing, he did not think I would do it.

He drops his gaze and falls into a chair. "Jordan, be a pal and bring me back some blood will you?" Jordan raises his chin in a light nod, but Kyle does not look back at us.

*　　*　　*

"Do you believe what the Astros say?" Jordan asks as the elevator doors lock us in. The slow elevator will take several minutes to carry us from the dungeon to the surface. If Jordan is speaking now, he has a good reason.

"The Astros say many things," I answer coldly, keeping my eyes forward. Already I am shifting back into Vegar Clara. I want to be her right now. While out of earshot of Kyle, Jordan might say anything. Being the Vegar will keep me focused, in control of myself.

"Do you believe what Liturgy says about *us*?" There is no doubt in my mind that *us* means Jordan and Clara. This past year, he has done well at maintaining the boundaries of our alliance without letting sentiment take control. Now that we are alone together, he is making his move. I close my eyes to clear my head.

He is a Guard and not built like a Slayer. Jordan hides his emotions better than the other Guards, but he has just as many. There are rules in Krisenica that prevent situations like this. We keep to our divisions. You cannot love someone when you do not understand them. I do not understand what he wants from me. Slayers do their job best when their emotions are distant from their thoughts and actions. Certain emotions may temporarily fuel passion in a fight, but a clear head will see you to the end of any confrontation.

Jordan is putting me in an impossible position, yet he pursues the conversation. "Has it been so many years that you have forgotten our youth?" Jordan's voice cracks a little, startling me. I instinctively turn toward him but catch myself before I move too far.

"That was many lifetimes ago," I say, facing forward again.

"That is not what I asked." Jordan's voice is still weak, forcing me to consider what he is asking me.

In my two thousand years on Earth, Astros prophecies have always come true. There are scrolls upon scrolls of prophecies that have come to be. Even when they quarrel among themselves, the Astros are able to discern the right path. Because we are only privy to a fraction of their prophecies, there are whisperings that the Astros cannot be trusted. That it is the Astros that keep us waiting on this planet, living lifetime after lifetime, when they have the power to take us anywhere in the universe. I do not believe those rumors.

"I remember every moment we spent together, but I cannot take a Guard for a mate. Still, if the prophecy about the Architect and their Guard is true, then Liturgy has chosen the only Guard that stands a chance at changing my mind." We are close to the top, and our time alone is running out. I pivot and look up at Jordan. "Liturgy is never wrong, but as I told Kyle, we can still choose."

Emotion ripples across his face in conflict. Gently, he reaches out, brushing his fingers against my cheek. "You are the Vegar. You can take whatever you want."

The elevator doors opens, and I spin away, striding toward the Litmar wing. With every step, I let Jordan fade into the place where I bury what little emotion I still have. Business first.

The Litmar wing is my least favorite place in Krisenica. Mostly because I cannot stand Litmars. They oversee the day-to-day business and handle most governing decisions. The Council is only summoned for very important matters. Protocols are in place to ensure decision-making is swift and efficient. Litmars remind us of the rules and enforce them as needed. They are smart, organized, and have even less emotion than a Slayer.

Out of all the divisions in Krisenica, Litmars visit the human world least. The older Litmars still retain the appearance of Lymerians from the dark ages: sharp teeth, yellow eyes, and ashy skin. Of course, the more surges we have, the more humanlike qualities we produce in our young. Nevertheless, Litmars remain the least adapted of our kind.

The commanders of each division regularly report to Farrell, Keeper of the Litmars, to answer questions and receive assignments. Samuel, a Slayer captain, has been reporting in my place. Skipping meetings with Farrell is one consolation of Liturgy, as I despise the man.

Krisenica's main communication room is housed in the Litmar wing. It oversees all things in and around Krisenica. Watching these screens allows the Litmars to investigate any law breaking, though such actions are rare. More importantly, they aid in the protection of Krisenica and every living soul inside. Both Guard gymnasiums and Slayer caves have similar technology, albeit on a smaller scale.

Litmars rely on Dormant reports to monitor farther into the human world. Astros may be called upon by Litmars to tell them what they *see.* Other Litmars spend their days watching screens in the communication room, taking notes with ink and quill. Using technology to monitor Lymerians and humans is perfectly acceptable to the Litmars, but a typewriter is blasphemy. Many rooms in the Litmar wing exist only to hold the endless scrolls of information.

There is also a senate room where Litmar leaders convene as needed. Only Litmars can hold office, and only they can vote each other into office—they are a species unto themselves. Most Lymerians care little for their games. We follow rules written thousands of years ago. The majority of Litmar negotiations pertain to the placement of Dormants, the largest division. Farrell takes great pleasure in moving Dormants around like chess pieces. Dormant placement matters little to the rest of us.

When human world affairs force us to intervene, Litmars act on behalf of the Astros to send Slayers, and occasionally Guards, where they are needed. They do not have enough imagination to significantly alter the affairs of humans. They are a soundboard to the real government of Krisenica—the Astros. It is rare, but Astros do speak on their own behalf when absolutely necessary.

"Vegar." Farrell's voice, a nasally growl, is unmistakable. "Up for a breather? How good of you to stop by."

Farrell was first elected Keeper when I was a child. He is as smart as we come and effectively charming when the occasion calls for it—

although when you live as long as we do, you cannot hide who you really are. I suppose the Litmars like him just as he is, or they would not continue to elect him.

He once tried to remove the position of Vegar, citing a Vegar held the power to tear the Lymerians in two. Slayers follow the command of their Vegar, not the Litmars. To a Slayer, only one Lymerian ranks above the Vegar—the Slayer that occupies a seat on the Council. I like to believe the Astros would interfere far before a calamity such as a rebellious Vegar could occur.

Farrell is strategizing with his favorite commander, Isaac, who is in charge of the Guards. Isaac is old like Farrell, but I like him. He is one of the few Lymerians with patches of gray in his hair and wrinkles upon his skin. Even I must admit they are a good fit as they work to decide which Guards are assigned wards and which are simply given posts. Their eyes scan two dozen pages of lists scattered on a large table, giving nods in agreement or silence in disagreement. Words are reserved for rare occasions when neither will budge. They have been a team longer than my existence.

Although Farrell has given me acknowledgement, as my post demands, I stay silent out of respect for Isaac. They are not finished.

"We can get back to this later—the Vegar's time is even more precious than usual." Isaac rises and our eyes meet. He understands respect. We both nod and he leaves.

"Report," I say, without looking at Farrell. I am not in the mood to play nice, though to be fair, I am never nice. The sooner he starts talking, the sooner I can get to my Slayers. Farrell stops handling the papers on his desk. In my peripheral vision, I see him glaring up at me. Perhaps he is thinking of a way to gain the upper hand. Farrell's yellow eyes stare up at me for several seconds before he remembers that Liturgy has made me even more untouchable than I was before.

"Few changes, here or in the human world. Cleanup following Liturgy was successful." He pauses, no doubt looking for a sign of discomfort from me. "The stewards have resumed their regular routine."

"All of them?"

"All of them." Farrell raises an eyebrow at the same time the side of his mouth twitches, threatening to smile. Farrell rarely smiles, because when he does, his entire profile changes. He goes from a respectable-looking prolific leader to an unhinged madman, manic even. It is a face one never forgets. I have seen it twice.

"Liturgy has already begun to change you, Vegar," Farrell says dismissingly. I do not rise to his taunting. Let him try to rattle me. He lets his words sink in before continuing. "I have seen many Liturgies in my time. Unlike you, I have always kept a keen eye on Architects and Votaries."

Farrell goes quiet, staring at the wall, eyes lost in his own memories. His features morph into near pleasantness, intriguing me for the first time in two millennia. The moment passes just as quickly as it comes, and the true Farrell starts talking again.

"The entire situation is unprecedented. A Vegar as Architect? Who do you really have down there?" Farrell's voice darkens, which confirms what I have already been thinking. This Liturgy is different. He knows I cannot speak of it.

"Is there anything else to report, Keeper?" I ask, finally making eye contact. Let him gaze into my eyes and know nothing has changed since I fought for my place as Vegar. It has been many moons since I visited Nadir, but my eyes still obey my command and shift.

"That is all," he says, and I leave.

On my way to the court, I see Jordan outside of the main gymnasium. He and his mate are breaking away from the rest of the Guards. Karina has her arms wrapped around his waist while he leads her away. I think about his eagerness to come above ground, and the smallest whisper of anger escapes me.

Such a small shift in my emotions could never be detected by a normal Lymerian. Perhaps an Astro, but none other. Jordan stops and looks right at me. Our eyes meet, and his widen with shame as he lurches away from Karina. I force myself to start walking again. Jordan can do whatever he wants. He does not belong to me and can choose to stay with his mate.

As I walk, I think about Farrell's words. He has witnessed every Liturgy and as Keeper, knows every participant. It changes everyone, but this soon? Who I am in the dungeons will not be who I am here. I move faster, trying to get as far away as I can from Farrell, Jordan, and Karina. It is not like me to run, but I need to be with the Slayers. I need to be the one thing that cannot change about me—Vegar.

The court is close, full of Slayers training and preparing for the next assignment. Their scents hit me, each one unique and distinct. I am home. They know I am coming as well. All of their conversations stop as they move themselves into two long parallel lines. One by one, their footsteps cease until the only steps anyone can hear are from my boots. *Click, click, click.*

There is no door to the court, just an archway that reaches thirty feet high and forty feet across. The Slayers' lines flank the entrance, forming a walkway down the court. Bright light brilliantly reflects off the white walls. This is the heaven humans so often write about. Affection for the Slayers, this room, and everything we stand for begins to tingle its way through me. I bury it instantly and keep my face stone as I survey my Slayers.

"You," I say to Gemma, a petite but fierce fighter. She steps forward, half grinning. "Choose two others." Gemma's grin widens. Wordlessly she nods in the direction of Evan and Tyler, Slayers from the last surge. They step forward, and the rest of the group breaks formation to give us room.

Gemma moves in to strike first while Tyler and Evan circle. With one arm, I brush away her attack, then Tyler's and Evan's. They fight individually, assuming three on one is enough to wear me down or pressure me into a mistake. This is not the way. I push my speed and eject each of them in different directions. All three Slayers bound back to their feet effortlessly.

"Do not fight as three, fight as one!" I shout.

Small Gemma easily maneuvers between Evan and Tyler, assisting them with attacks and working twice as hard. She will tire first, lessening their advantage.

"No!" My voice thunders, and they all stop.

A few heads turn toward the archway. Jordan is standing between two Slayers. Their positions indicate they have not laid hands on him, but they are blocking him from moving any further into the court. With my Slayer's eyes, I take him in. He is confused and flushed from running. Whatever Jordan felt from the other side of Krisenica made him believe I was in danger.

"Let him be," I say to the Slayers blocking him. Then I nod to Gemma to continue.

This time each attack is calculated—thinking as one. Evan and Tyler move on me first with a stream of hits, never targeting the same body part twice. It wears me down. They are waiting for a window, a slipup so they can gain the advantage. Jordan's presence breaks my concentration and for less than a second, I lose focus. Evan sees and strikes under my left arm. Gemma's boot hits my right side before I can recover from Evan's blow. Then Tyler from the front and repeat.

Bruises on top of bruises spread over me as blood moistens my hair and face, but my senses stay alert. There is trouble outside the four of us. Concern fuels me to reach deep within to a place where my champion lives. I throw away the three of them and wheel around to see Jordan trying to move through a wall of Slayers.

"Do not lay hands on him. He is a Guard of Liturgy. No one can touch him. It is the law." I speak calmly to them from a place of duty, leaving no trace of my growing affection for Jordan. I am the Vegar making sure my Slayers follow our laws.

I whirl back around, turning my back on Jordan. "Too many times, we fight as individuals," I shout, moving to address anyone I can catch with my eyes. "Slayers go their own way in battle because we rarely meet an enemy that matches our strength. When that day comes, we shall be ready." I take a few steps back to indicate that is all for today. "Samuel," I say, keeping my voice low.

The court is where we train and spend most of our time. Where we sleep, eat, and work are beyond the court through the caves. As I pass Jordan, I briefly nod to let him know he should follow me out of the court. Samuel catches up to us with a portfolio beneath his arm and a cloth on the other. When we reach one of the work rooms, Samuel goes in, and I turn to Jordan.

"I will be done in a minute. Then we can go back."

Jordan does not reply. Instead, he moves to stand against the wall opposite the small window of the work room. Work rooms are all sound proof. Jordan will not be able to hear what we say, but he will be watching us.

"Report," I say, shutting the door. Samuel hands me the cloth. I take it and rub away what blood I can from my face and hands.

"It's been quiet. The Litmars don't want to make any moves while you are away and Angelica's disappearance is so recent. As you are aware, the family doesn't pose a threat, but there were others we couldn't get to—those that knew about the relationship between Angelica and Merrick, for example. Dormants are keeping their ears open and reporting anything we can't get our hands on here. Names, dates, pictures, and locations are here."

I nod and take the portfolio from him. "Continue the training that I have started today. No more one-on-one fights. This is our new method, and I want your full support."

Samuel's expression changes, questioning, but I will not explain myself. His curiosity morphs quickly to seriousness as he deliberately moves out of sight of the window. Jordan stiffens, appearing unexpectedly dangerous. He does not like losing sight of Samuel.

"Can we talk about something else, Clara?"

I sift through the portfolio, operating as casually as a Vegar is capable. When I do not answer, Samuel steps too close to me, in Jordan's view again. Gently his fingers graze against mine.

"Things have changed," I bark. Samuel ignores me, rooting his fingers to mine, making me flush. His scent reminds me of dry Earth and the hot sun, even after all these years, a sigh escapes me. Africa will always be my true home, the home of my youth.

I stand up and pull my hand away from his.

"You won't be down there forever. Those years are nothing to our kind. You will return soon enough." He pauses, sensing my distance. "We were just getting started." Samuel is right, but my heart was never truly in it, and it certainly is not now.

"Liturgy can't make you do anything you don't want to do, Clara. You still get to choose." His words echo the ones I said to Kyle not long ago. Samuel is familiar, and he is home. Not long ago I surrendered to his smooth ebony touch and his fighter's eyes, but that was before Angelica.

"It is not Liturgy," I lie, walking to the door. Samuel uses his speed and blocks my way, forcing me to look him in the eyes.

"If that's true, then why not? Your mate left us years ago, and you have to move on." Our recent moments of intimacy allow me to forgive him once for speaking so out of turn. Samuel sees his mistake in my eyes and says no more. He kisses me softly, and once again I wish she had not heard my voice in her head.

"Take care of them," I say as I open the door.

Jordan is gone. With my quarters so near, I stop to change my bloody clothes then hurry to find Jordan. He is at the edge of the tunnels that lead to the court and Slayer quarters. He walks shoulder to shoulder with me, putting up a unified front for anyone who might see us, but his anger cannot hide from me. Minutes tick by on the elevator in silence. Then he sucks in a breath.

"You make the rules in the dungeons, but you will respect me on the surface." Surprisingly his voice is calm, but then again, he rarely raises his voice in anger. This declaration takes me aback. No matter what the Astros foretell, neither of us have entered into an agreement. I owe him nothing.

"You should not have followed me into the court. It is no place for a Guard."

"This is not about the court."

"What is it about then?" Jordan glances up and runs his hand over his short hair, his perfected mask slipping away. The elevator jerks to a stop. As soon as the doors open, we start walking.

"A few hours ago, you said I am the only Guard for you. And we both know that before we had divisions, it was you and me. You chose me out of everyone. You were sent with the Slayers, I to the Guards, and that was that. You were so fixated on following the order of things."

"Order is the only way!" I shout, careless of my surroundings now that we are back below the surface. Being in the dungeons is becoming familiar, natural even. We are safe here, and I can scream and yell and feel. "Do not act as if you are suffering. The first thing you did on the surface was find your mate."

"Gone three hours to come back bickering like Dormants. Nice plan, Jordan. Good thing I'm staying right here." Kyle swivels his chair to face us, temporarily snapping us out of our argument. "Did Jordan do that to you?" Kyle asks, laughing as he eyes my bruises. I did not take blood to heal. Jordan turns back to me, ignoring Kyle.

"I went to Karina to make a clean break of it. Which went to shit because you showed up. Instead of giving her the explanation she deserves, I went running after you. It could be months before I make it back to the surface to explain my actions. Then, right in my face, you and whatever his name—"

"I did not ask you to come after me," I say weakly. It is all I can manage to say because I am ashamed. This conversation is turning into something I am not ready for.

"Come on, Clara. I do not have any control over this. When that girl accepted your command, it bound Kyle to her and me to you."

The room goes quiet, except for our three steady heartbeats. Kyle has no quips, Jordan is spent, and I am at a loss for words. Quite simply, I do not feel the same passion he does. Too much time has passed since our youth.

"Karina has been my mate for hundreds of years, but when I am with her, I think of you." Jordan slumps into a chair, letting every muscle go slack.

"Good times. Does this mean you forgot the blood?"

"Shit." Jordan exhales, giving Kyle an apologetic glance. Kyle grins and pats Jordan on his back.

"It's fine. Next time."

"Why are you in such a good mood?" I ask accusingly. Does our quarreling make him happy?

Kyle points to the screen. "She isn't asleep."

Jordan and I both move closer to the screen. Kyle leaves the room, giving us space though I am not sure that will do any good. Angelica is sitting quietly, calm and awake. I exhale in relief and look to Jordan. An apology and promise hover on my lips. I am sorry and will never touch Samuel again. Jordan speaks first.

"I am not just your favorite Guard," he says quietly, reaching to take my hand. "I cannot stand the thought of his hands on yours." He rubs his fingers over mine, one by one as if to erase every trace of Samuel. I squeeze my eyes shut, commanding myself to hold my ground. Being Vegar comes with a steep price. Even if Liturgy permits a Slayer to choose a Guard, it will weaken my position. Gently, I detach myself from him, pulling back every emotion I let loose moments ago and sucking it down to my depths. My eyes are as cold as I can manage when I speak.

"Take the first shift."

Chapter 8

Angelica

A few hours have gone by since Clara left, and I'm already bored. Refusing to use my new strength means less ways to entertain myself. I could sleep, letting time pass in the blink of eye, but the year lost in dreams haunts me. I do not want to sleep anymore.

When you are long-lived, doesn't time pass faster? I never asked Merrick how time felt for him. Maybe a month feels like an hour, a quick trip to the doctor. I give it a try, shutting my eyes and imagining my last visit to Dr. Mackenzie's office. There are lots of seats, but I'm the only one waiting. Betty glances at me from her reception desk every few minutes with a reassuring smile that says *You're next, just a little longer.*

The office is crisper than I remember. My mind fills in the details of the room with pieces of memories I assumed long lost—blue chairs, beige walls, a fish tank, worn magazines, cheap tissues. Every time something new appears into the room, I instantly remember that I've seen it here before. This must be them, something they changed about me. My memory, the human one, is terrible. Entire pieces of my life are missing, yet I'd bet my allowance that Betty has a pair of pearl earrings and a yellow top that she wore the last time I was at the doctor.

I abandon the office, deciding to keep busy by testing out my new memory. Everything is neatly stored and easy to find in this brain. As soon as I think of a date, place, person or conversation, the setting springs to life behind my lids.

Watching myself through Lymerian eyes, I am less than even ordinary. In the orphanage, the sisters always gave passing grades. Public school was challenging, and I was far behind. At the time, I attributed the deficit to the orphanage, nuns doubling as teachers. Eventually I would catch up, I always thought.

In these memories, I see my face pitted against the other children—happy, thriving children that understood the task in front of them. My face is scrunched in concentration or gazing out the window, ignoring the assignment entirely. Here, I am inadequate to my peers with no one to blame but myself.

Truth be told, my mind isn't the only thing that is less than ordinary. I am pale, plain, thin, and tall. Rebecca glows next to an ordinary Angelica. In all my memories, the only person that fits this homely Angelica is my homely friend Janice. It makes sense—we come from the same place.

Knowing this should make me feel sad, but I feel nothing. Even Rebecca's warm smile fails to ignite one spark of the love I know I have for her. Human parts still clanging around inside of me warn that this isn't right. *Why are you accepting this so easily*? I look down and pull my hair to where I can see it. This hair is not the right hair color, and my skin looks even more pale than I remember. *Facts*. They are just facts without any emotion attached.

Clara's blood may make my memory sharper, body stronger, but it has taken away my emotions. Or did it begin the moment I realized I was one of them? The sorrow I felt moments before waking up is gone.

I recall the memories from the days I was kept captive in this very room. I see myself terrified, cold, and full of guilt. Guilt for leaving loved ones without explaining and fear for Merrick and me. As I sit in the same cell alone and completely awake this time, I feel nothing.

I'm not worried about Rebecca, and I don't miss Vic. The thought of Clara coming back doesn't scare me. Honestly, I want her to come back, my body already desiring more blood. I'm not mad that I'm not human anymore. I'm not sad that Merrick is dead. Thoughts and memories are now facts and nothing more.

One by one, I think about the people I'm sure I care about. For hours, maybe days, I replay the most important moments from my life, but nothing ever stirs in me. Every detail of our time together is neatly stored in my mind, a mere collection of data that no longer hold any significance to me. I could close my eyes, ready to fall back into the place where I can rewrite memories full of emotion.

No. No more sleep.

My days pass in an endless waking cycle. Think of a memory, try to recreate the feeling in the memory, give up, consider sleep, refuse to sleep, repeat. Eventually I stumble upon something important—Merrick's laugh. Merrick was Lymerian and had emotions. I should have emotions too.

Before I can stop myself, I am caught in a stream of memories with Merrick. Merrick wanted children, wanted them with me someday. We talked about that a lot. The little girl we daydreamed into life had dark hair just like his and my blue eyes. I can see her clearly in my mind as she skips through an open field wearing a purple dress. The sun blazes in a sky the same shade of blue as her eyes. She turns to me and smiles. My heart flutters. It only lasts a second, but I would recognize that feeling anywhere—love.

Good. I have to keep this up. Instead of bringing up old memories, I imagine the future I lost with all the people I love. Vic finally meeting Merrick. They shake hands. Rebecca holding a perfect baby. All of us, Peter, Judy, Merrick, Vic, Rebecca and me, sitting down to eat at our dinner table.

Click. The noise triggers an elegant stream of thoughts through my upgraded brain: *eyes to the door, stay still, another* click*, it's a rhythm, heel on stone, someone is coming, Clara.* I relax, unaware of the tension until it releases. Absentmindedly, I count her steps when I should be making a plan.

If I had emotions, I would know how I feel and react accordingly. Scared would be an appropriate response—they are dangerous with precise rules and strict laws. Laws that killed Merrick. Anger would be fitting too, for the same reason. They pretty much killed me, and they definitely killed my future. Instead, I don't think I care about who is coming, what they want, or what they will do to me.

Just as I'm about to hit five hundred, the steps stop. The unmistakable sound of a lock sliding is next. When the door finally opens, it thunders like it took the weight of ten men to heave it just a few inches. My visitor—the petite, ghostly woman—looks exactly the same as she did in her other visits. Head-to-toe black, tight-fitted clothing with black heeled boots. Even though her hair is pulled high on her head, it still reaches to her mid back. It is black, shiny, and strong. Her face is round, lips thin, eyes deadly. Everything about her is impressive.

Clara flicks her small wrist against the massive door, and it slams shut. As promised, she pulls another small vial from her pocket and tosses it. The bottle arcs, starting its descent too soon. My mind knows that I need to move fast, faster than I know how, to catch the vial before it falls and breaks. There won't be another vial. When I move to grab it, it doesn't feel like I'm moving fast, but I reach it. I show restraint this time and remove the cork first. With a steady hand, I gently tip the precious tube back into my mouth. Immediately I feel its affects and am even less concerned about my emotions.

Clara holds her hand out, and I obediently return the empty vial. "Lymerian senses are a hundred times more sensitive than human. One of the reasons you spend your time in isolation is so you will not be overwhelmed by the stimuli. You could hear me approaching. The way I walk is unique to me. In time, you will be able to tell the difference between my stride and all others and learn to ignore what you do not need. Listen hard."

I listen as she walks around the room, picking up the pattern of her heart. It beats in synchronicity with her stride, slower than a human heart.

"Scent. Everyone has a particular aroma. This will be a most powerful tool when distinguishing friend from stranger." *Merrick.*

She smelled like him before. I inhale deeply, but there is no trace of him on her now. Had it all been my imagination? Clara turns her head sharply to one of the walls and sighs. I look, but see nothing.

"How do you feel?"

Blankly I stare at her. Why would they care how I feel? Clara's gaze tells me she is about to lose patience with me, so I tell the truth.

"I don't feel anything."

A shadow crosses her face like she's actually concerned for me. She steps close and focuses her eyes on mine. Lightly she lifts my wrist to her ear, sets it back down and snickers.

"What?" I ask, wanting to understand what she does.

"Shall I show you?"

I stay silent, skeptical of her methods. She is one of them, and I don't trust her. Yet curiosity moves my head upward in a nod. Then I am across the cell, gasping for air. She kicked me in the gut. It happened in a fraction of a second, but I remember each movement. Clara spun, her foot met my gut and propelled me into the wall, and I crumbled to the floor where I now crouch, staring at her in disbelief.

"How do you feel now?"

"Angry," I reply without thinking, but it's the truth. I am very angry. Almost angry enough to fight back. As a human, I never wanted to fight back, and hardly ever felt angry at anyone. This is an emotion, but it's the wrong one. I stand and walk back to Clara. "Why am I angry?"

"Because I hit you. You have emotion. You are welcome."

"Is anger the only emotion I can feel?" Clara doesn't answer me right away. She's thinking about something. Her eyes look beyond me.

"Of course not," she finally says. "Anger is the easiest emotion to feel. Why do you not sleep?"

"I'm not tired."

"You will be in this cell for a while. Physically, your body needs the rest. The blood I give you is minimal, and your youth demands much sustenance. Mentally, you need your dreams. Your brain is not fully developed. Dreams help." I only have a few seconds to let her words sink in before she adds, "I want you to sleep, Angelica."

* * *

"Do you like it?" Rebecca asks as she scrambles past me into my new room. It's August 1954, the day of my adoption.

"Rebecca, did you know this would happen to me?" I ask from the doorway, ignoring her attempt to follow the memory. Sometimes Rebecca just knew things, little things, like knowing when the rain was going to stop or announcing that Vic wasn't coming home moments before he would call to say so. This was Judy's reason for homeschooling her. They were all very protective of her, even Vic. Part of me always thought that I'd been adopted to be Rebecca's friend, not that I would have loved her any less if that were true. I was the only one that let Rebecca breathe. We snuck out together and danced in the rain once. Another time, I took her to the zoo, and we pet the goats. She loved that. Now, I hope dream Rebecca is as intuitive as in real life.

"I knew you would leave," Rebecca says very seriously, sounding years older. Emotions come and I welcome them. It feels like years have gone by, instead of weeks, since I felt love in my heart. I feel like myself again. Whether or not it's a dream, I don't care. Rebecca is my sister, and if I reach for her she will feel as real as the last time I touched her.

Rebecca moves over to the window with a book in her hand and the memory is back where it belongs. I follow and sit opposite her to gaze at my tree. When I turn back to Rebecca, Vic is sitting next to her, both asleep, both at my side. We should have had a lifetime together, but now I will never see them again.

The heartache I feel is real, and it reaches deep into my soul.

Chapter 9

Clara

Year two proves to be as stressful as year one, but for different reasons. Visits to Angelica are regulated to thirty-day intervals and fall into an easy pattern. She feeds, and we have lessons covering a broad range of Lymerian topics. The breadth of information is far reaching, though we have yet to speak of Liturgy. Angelica absorbs everything, asking questions only when necessary.

After my rejection, Jordan ignores me, refusing to utter even a single word in passing. His silence is the greatest hardship of all, though I could never admit that to anyone. Kyle becomes the unlikely thread holding our trinity together, for Angelica if nothing else. Having already lost Jordan, I commit to controlling my temper with Kyle.

Whenever I feel myself losing control, I return to the surface where I am always in control. While my visits are erratic, Jordan goes at regular intervals, bringing fresh blood for Kyle and reeking of Karina's scent. He did not give her up as he once planned.

Kyle and Jordan develop a routine in my absences. When I am on the surface, with Angelica, or pretending to sleep, they talk about Liturgy. I first became suspicious after returning from a trip to the caves to find Kyle bubbling with new ideas. In my paranoia, I stopped sleeping to eavesdrop. When I was sure their conversations were for the advancement of the process, I let myself sleep once again.

Knowing Jordan is well intentioned does nothing to dull the ache of being excluded. We should be three, and Liturgy is punishing me because we are broken. I denied Jordan's affection by doing what I do best, burying my emotions. Now I suffer for it. Angelica suffers too. Whispering suggestions to Kyle while I am away is not enough. Jordan's part is bigger in this. Even so, Kyle and I make the best of it.

After each session with Angelica, we confer in the viewing room. I tell them what they cannot observe through the monitors or glean from the speakers. Immediately after, Jordan leaves for the surface, pretending to have no further interest. Kyle and I remain for hours talking about her.

Kyle wants to know every change with her since the previous visit, no matter how minute. How her features shift when she talks, the volume of her voice, the paleness of her skin, how many times she blinks—everything matters to him. These kinds of questions do not bother me, and I answer easily.

We exchange ideas about what her behavior means. As a human, she was frightened and hysterical at times. During the first visit, she was ruled completely by emotions, and her instinct was to fight. Since then, she has shown no emotion and appears more and more complacent every time I see her.

My theory is that her Lymerian mind is blocking emotions so that she can adapt and survive in these new circumstances. Kyle is concerned that my blood is overtaking her natural disposition. He sees me as a Slayer, a Vegar without emotions, and feeding on my blood must be why Angelica is behaving this way. He wants me to give her his blood instead. I have considered his argument closely, but there is one thing that does not fit. Feeding on my blood should alter Angelica's appearance, at least briefly, yet it does not. She remains in complete contrast to me. Angelica is light where I am darkness. My blood cannot overtake her genes, even momentarily.

After we analyze everything from the most recent visit, we plan the next. Then we review the plan periodically throughout the month to make sure everything is still sound. Things are changing between us. Seeing my ways have not ruined her builds some trust with Kyle.

I no longer make all the decisions either. Instead, we work as a true team.

Now that Angelica stays awake, Kyle is much changed. Her voice keeps him calm. Without the constant worry, Kyle falls back into his old, strange self. He is kind, soft-spoken, and even laughs sometimes.

Kyle's newest obsession is guessing what division she will be assigned to. He is thinking beyond Liturgy. Mates must be from the same division, except in very specific circumstances that are quite rare. Guards with Guards, Litmars with Litmars, and so on. Since Liturgy is of an order above ordinary Lymerian laws, it carries one of the exceptions. Those chosen for Liturgy may have a mate from their division or from their Liturgy. It matters not if Angelica is a Slayer or a Litmar, she may still choose Kyle for her mate. In the unlikely event that she is a Guard, then the chances of her favoring him increase substantially. Since Lymerians are fiercely loyal to their divisions, no Guard will choose Angelica as a mate until Kyle has a mate as well. If Angelica is a Guard, she chooses Kyle or no one.

"If she were a Slayer, she'd want to fight, right?"

I am going to see Angelica soon, so Kyle and I are going over the plan one final time. Kyle is getting off subject—again.

"She fought in the beginning," I remind him. "And she fought for her life at Liturgy."

"Yeah, but either could point to her being a Guard."

This grabs my attention. If Kyle has a theory related to this, I have never heard him tell it. "Explain."

"Some Guards can be just as vicious as Slayers if they are defending someone very important to them." He says the second part quietly, admitting that for his theory to be true, she really cared about Merrick. I replay the night in my mind. It is true that Angelica's entire demeanor changed when Anubis started to ask about Merrick. Her fear lessened, and her propensity for violence and action increased.

"Maybe, maybe not Kyle. There is much we do not understand. There could be many reasons for her behavior, and it is our job to figure them out." He nods and sits down while I get up to leave.

"She's not a Slayer. Your blood would bring it out of her." He says it more to himself than to me, but I do not agree.

"Fighting me would be foolish. I would never be so foolish and neither would she." There are many different kinds of Slayers, though I do not expect Kyle to understand. It is too early to discount any division save Astro. "I am going to my room for a while before I see her."

"You don't have to tell her today," Kyle says unexpectedly. "There's plenty of time still." Kyle's eyes are kind, so kind that I am not sure if he is thinking of me or her. It is possible that my next discussion with Angelica will be just as difficult for me as it will be for her.

"I do not wish to delay it," I say neutrally, trying not to give away how difficult I expect this next session to be for Angelica.

Kyle is still eyeing me. "She's not ready for the truth, Clara. Please wait."

"The longer we wait, the worse it is. We are building trust by being as honest as possible at this point in Liturgy." After a long minute, Kyle nods.

How different this conversation would have gone a year ago. Kyle and I are both changing, trusting each other.

* * *

"You did not sleep this past month."

Angelica takes the vial and drinks my blood, avoiding my eyes. It is clear she does not want to say anything else about it, so I move on.

"During the last several months, we have discussed many things. You know about Krisenica, the Lymerian body, some history, the divisions. Yet you know very little about why you are here. Today, I am going to tell you *why.*" This holds her attention, putting a light back into her eyes for just a moment.

"Did Merrick ever speak of Liturgy to you?" A quick shake of the head. *No*. "All beings have laws or rules that organize, judge, and give purpose to them. Lymerians have such laws of course, but we have another set of laws as well. They are called the Laws of Liturgy, one of the few things given to us by the original Lymerian inhabitants of this planet." I pause. There is much to understand here.

"Were you here before humans?"

"Of course not. Humans evolved on this planet." She stays silent, so I keep going. "The Laws of Liturgy were written by Astros long ago."

"The psychics," she says quietly.

"Psychic is a human concept and should not be used to describe an Astro. As I have explained to you before, the Astros are the smallest in number—the rarest kind of Lymerian. Their blood can never risk dilution. They are quite literally of the stars. Nearly all Astros that first arrived on this planet are still alive."

Her eyes lose focus as she plucks one of her many questions to ask first. "How many of you have died?"

"I do not know the number. Most of the first travelers died from old age, others on the battlefield, and some by our own hand. We do not live forever, just much longer than a human. If our injuries are severe enough or we cannot access blood to heal, we will die. This planet provides the perfect habitat to sustain organisms, creating a variety of life on Earth. But life on Earth is brief for most inhabitants."

"Why do you live longer?"

"We live longer because our cells regenerate rapidly, a hundred times faster than a human. Lymerian DNA evolved on a much harsher planet than Earth. It had to regenerate quickly to survive. There, our lifespans were shorter than a human's on Earth. Because of our short lifespans, it took many generations of Astros to piece together the path of our future. They predicted our future lay in another planet, where we could live like kings."

"Earth," she says, sitting back. Merrick never explained where we came from. He painted us as monsters he was trying to escape.

I push that thought away so I can continue. "The Astros disagree when it comes to Earth. Some believe our journey ends here, others believe it is merely a resting point."

"Because you live too long here."

"Precisely. This dilemma has plagued Lymerians since they first came to Earth. Most of the original Lymerians have died of age since coming to this planet, but no Lymerian born on Earth has died from old age."

"Is that why Lymerians want to become human?"

Everything stops around me at her words. I have not forgiven Merrick for wanting to be human. The moment passes, and I force myself back to the lesson, ignoring her question.

"Thousands of years ago, we learned very quickly that too much human blood weakened us, made us like humans. As the centuries passed, many chose to leave, permitted by the Astros at first. There was discord among them. As I said before, some do not believe Earth is where we belong. At one point, the majority of Astros wanted us to assimilate into the human race. The longer we stayed on Earth, the harder it became for us to reproduce and more Astros started to seek other paths.

"Their visions promised our salvation lay with the human race. If we upheld the Laws of Liturgy above all others, Lymerians would be saved. Robust humans were chosen for Liturgy, but few survived. Eventually the Astros could see the problem. Once the missing piece was discovered, everything fell into place. Liturgy became a common practice until our numbers were sufficient for the Astros and the Council. Now it is only done when it is necessary to replace one of our own kind.

"I'm here because you killed one of your own kind." Neither of us speak. We are both trapped in our minds, reliving the final moments of her human life and Merrick's Lymerian one. Merrick dies and Angelica takes his place for the preservation of Lymerians. "You didn't have to kill Merrick," she spits at me.

"Merrick lived many lifetimes and would have died trying to leave us." I make sure my voice stays calm. But it does not matter; her anger has surfaced.

"Why didn't you just let him go!" Angelica jumps up and stands over me. "What is one less Lymerian? You have plenty." She starts to pace, her mind spinning. "It was working. He was becoming more and more human. Why not just let him go?"

"If we let him go, we would have to let everyone go!" I shout back at her, surprised by my own veracity. She stops pacing, her Lymerian brain understanding what her heart cannot.

"Why don't all humans survive?" She folds her arms and leans against the wall defiantly.

"In order to survive, the human must have Lymerian lineage."

"I'm an orphan."

"But you were someone's child, and they had Lymerian ancestry."

Angelica is thinking, trying to find something in her memory that can confirm what I have said. I already know there is nothing.

"How could your Council possibly know?"

"Merrick made an interesting decision with you." Angelica tenses. "He gave you his blood."

"So we could stay ahead of all of you, so I would be strong enough to fight."

"Lymerian blood has no effect on a human, but it had an effect on you. It made you stronger, faster. Perhaps your Lymerian heritage is what drew him to you and you to him. At some point in your relationship, he started to suspect."

"That's enough," she says, moving across the room quickly.

"I am not done explaining Liturgy."

"I don't want to talk about it anymore." Angelica paces, her breathing getting faster, hands shaking. Her mind is jumping ahead in the story to the ultimate climax, and she suspects correctly. This is the part Kyle wanted to spare her from. The truth of her existence that will leave her riddled with guilt.

"It is hard to hear, I know, but you must listen. I must be absolutely clear on this point. For you to be one of us and move forward as a Lymerian, you must hear the words out loud."

Angelica stops pacing and faces me, steadying herself for the worst. This partial truth will hurt her, but is nothing compared to the real truth, the truth she is not ready to comprehend.

"He was executed because we knew you would live."

"Get out," she breaths, barely in control.

I turn on my heel and walk to the door, knowing we are done for now. The door closes with a click behind me, yet her sobs follow me down the hallway. They weaken me. If Kyle comes, I may not have the strength to stop him.

Once I know she cannot hear me and am out of view of any cameras, I stop to gather myself. I am shaking as emotions rise, spilling into every part of me. Kyle and Jordan cannot hear me, but soon they will come looking for me. *Stop this,* I think and use all my strength to steady my hands. Instead of gaining control over myself, the trembling worsens, and my breaths quicken in time with my racing heart. I fall to my knees, palms on the cold ground. The heaviness, guilt, and sadness become too much. I crumble into a small ball and silently weep. These tears are long overdue, because Slayers do not weep, especially their Vegar.

Telling Angelica this story has taken everything out of me. This is why I did not want this Liturgy. But fate is often times cruel. She may never forgive me for what we have done.

A noise breaks me from my trance, but I cannot move quickly enough to recover. Jordan kneels next to me. Wordlessly he pulls me into him, and I surrender. His presence instantly makes me feel better, stronger. Jordan does not try to soothe me. He knows I do not want his hands caressing my hair or little kisses on my head. We are not a pair of Dormants or humans. What I need is him to be strong while I fall apart, and that is exactly what he does. His unmovable embrace shields me until my emotions are spent. It is everything I need.

Back in the viewing room, Kyle is as wrecked as me. When we enter, he jumps to his feet, ready to unleash his anger. But after one look at me, his face manages to lose even more color. Out of habit we take our seats, speechless. Kyle, red eyed, stares at the floor. I am across from him, glaring my anger at the wall. Jordan is between us, facing the monitors.

"She was not ready," Kyle finally says quietly. "You were not ready." Though his tone is accusing, there is no fight in him.

"She will never forgive me when she learns the whole truth," I say.

"You are her Architect. She will understand when the time is right," Jordan says softly, eyes still on the screen. Kyle looks up at me, as if to echo Jordan, but he says nothing. Instead, he laughs. Jordan and I wear equally annoyed and confused stares.

"Jordan's right, Clara. Liturgy has twisted us in a few human years. Vegar Clara is broken hearted over the emotions of a human. Better yet, you actually care whether or not *I'm* upset with you. I'm a Guard, Clara, and you are the Vegar." He laughs, and I look at Jordan. "And Jordan stopped talking to you for a year because . . . honestly, I'm not even sure what happened up there. But you guys were only gone a couple hours."

When I think about everything like a Vegar and not an Architect, I get the joke. I do not laugh, but at least I understand why Kyle is. Jordan slowly exhales and cracks a smile, which is as good as laughing for him.

"Our emotions are tied together. The intensity is greater and being down here, so far from the others, is completely different." Jordan points a finger to the ceiling. "They cannot see us, cannot hear us, and definitely cannot tell us what to do. We are all we have."

Kyle nods. "We've got Angelica too—that's what I'm saying. She is just as much a part of this as the three of us are. I trust both of you, a hell of a lot more than I did even a year ago. Give her time. She will come around to us. I know it. She will forgive us when the time comes."

We look back to the screens, none of sure what to do next. Angelica is already pulling herself back together. "You two should get some sleep." Kyle smirks, eyes darting between the two of us.

"What is that supposed to mean?" I protest, but Jordan already has my hand in his, tugging slowly as he rises from his seat. Kyle's face is alit in triumph. If the Vegar is not strong enough to resist the influence of Liturgy, neither will Angelica. Kyle misunderstands. He has no idea how long I have carried a piece of Jordan in my heart. Liturgy cannot make you love someone. It chooses your best chance at forming bonds. Soft, happy Kyle with his easy smile and carefree nature—a match for Angelica? No. He is not her match, but he will be devoted, which is exactly what she needs. For now.

Clara. "I have to go back," I announce, dropping Jordan's hand and moving quickly down the long hallway.

Chapter 10

Angelica

I was wrong. I was wrong again and again. Sitting in a pool of my own tears, I know that my emotions never left me. They were hiding, appearing only in my dreams. Clara hit the right pressure points and everything erupted to the surface.

Part of me hates her for delivering the truth, but she didn't order Merrick's death. Logic is already sobering me, forcing emotion back undercover. "No!" I shout to the air, fighting the change inside me. I don't want to be like them. *Be mad,* my mind whispers to me. *Every day you are more like them and less like you.*

I can't give in to the plea because anger and tears are for helpless creatures. I am not helpless anymore. I am Lymerian. At my admission, the small piece of me still championing for my humanity shifts focus.

Clara gave you information—use it. I need to take this information and dissect it until I understand how this changes everything I thought I knew.

Meeting Merrick wasn't serendipitous. He was drawn to the Lymerian in me, not the less than ordinary girl living in my memories. It's probably why he told me as much as he did about the Lymerians without considering the risk he put me, a simple human, in. I was never a simple human.

The morsel of Lymerian suppressed in my DNA kept me apart from humans my whole life. When I finally met someone that had it too, I held on tight. Merrick felt right and nothing anyone said could change that. Time after time I brushed off Janice's warnings, euphoria clouding the dangers of our relationship.

Merrick was executed because they knew you would live. Clara's voice echoes in my head, urging me forward in this quest. For three days, they kept me in this cell when they should have finished me off. Instead they kept me alive hoping I would lead them to Merrick. Unless . . . *No.* Firmly I think the word as if it will erase the most logical chain of events. I close my eyes and reach back to the night they caught me.

I remember finding a place to camp, sheltered by low trees with a smooth floor. Merrick is away, looking for dinner. I'm so tired from our constant trek, I start to drift, head cushioned on my arms.

When I wake up, I'm in a stone cell with a barred door, and my hands are tied to a chair. One of them, a Lymerian, is staring at me from a few feet away. He is wearing a human police uniform, but I can tell he's not human. Merrick told me what to look for. His facial features are slightly off from a human: large eyes that slant down, wide nose and sharper cheekbones. Most of his exposed skin is painted to appear like human flesh, but flashes of gray mark where the makeup has worn off.

He questions me for hours. Luckily, the only thing I have to pretend to be ignorant about is my knowledge that he is an alien. I do not know where I am or, his favorite question, where Merrick is hiding. Eventually, he unties my hands, takes the chair, and leaves me in the cell—for three days.

I break free of the memory and glance around my cell—the same cell. My human eyes were useless in this cell; my human lungs barely better suited. Now my vision reaches the stone ceiling and legs itch to scale the walls.

Focus on finding the truth, my inner voice nudges.

What truth? The truth is, I don't remember being caught or being brought to Krisenica. It's possible that Merrick and I were captured and brought back to Krisenica together. Everything that happened to me from the moment I was caught was done because they wanted me to be his replacement.

"Clara," I murmur. I want answers, but I also want Clara.

The wall. That voice, my instinct, thinks someone is watching me. All I see is a wall.

"I should not have left before." Clara's cold voice jumbles my focus. She's close. Moments later the door swings open, and Clara's small form appears.

Before the bit of human left inside me can argue, I let myself feel relief. In that moment, it doesn't matter that she is one of them, that I am one of them, that Merrick is dead, or that I will never see my family again. I'm not alone here. Knowing for sure that it isn't going to be me against them for the rest of eternity, or however long human converts like me get to live, lifts a weight I hadn't realized I'd been carrying.

"Will you finish?" I ask, needing to know the rest of Liturgy. Clara gives a small nod, leaving the door open as she joins me, sitting for the first time.

"Astros are unlike anything I have seen in all my years on Earth. I have seen many prophecies made come true. Such precise predictions that none can question their ability. When it was foretold that Liturgy would save our race, *all* Lymerians obeyed.

"Liturgy, however, is much more complex than finding a suitable human to assimilate into Lymerian. There are twenty-five laws. In short, they say that each Liturgy ceremony shall name three to guide, protect, and mentor the one to be. An Architect to bridge the two worlds, two lives, two species. Two Guards, one to protect and one to preserve. Four as one shall build a new life and erase old ones."

Clara pauses and I repeat every word in my head to make sure I understand it all. "You are the Architect," I say, then add, "Where are the Guards?"

"Not far, never far from either of us." She looks to the spot on the wall that beckoned me moments ago. Clara's face softens and for a moment she looks like an ordinary woman.

"Who am I?" An Architect, two Guards, and me.

"You are my Votary, which once was a title of great importance among Lymerians. When speaking to me, this is how others will refer to you. If I am not there, they will simply call you the replacement. Kyle, Jordan, myself, and anyone else you ever hold dear will call you Angelica."

I suck in a breath, absorbing the shock of learning which Lymerians were chosen to protect me. Strangers that will eventually be *dear* to me.

"How can I trust them?" Or her. Why would any Lymerian want to erase their old life for one with me, a second-class Lymerian? Votary *used* to be a title of importance. Not anymore.

"We are not assigned to be part of Liturgy. It is a calling. No one but the Astros really understand the powers that drive Liturgy, but we have all seen those powers in action. For instance, when you heard my voice in your head and did what I ordered." Clara pauses in case I want to ask a question. I always knew it had been her voice in my head, just not why.

"Everyone was whispering to you in the arena. All of them beckoning you to listen to their command." The swarm of whispers swirl in my head. Clara goes on. "When you did not move, their whispers grew louder." I remember the wave of growing voices. "I stayed silent. It is against the rules, but I had my reasons. Eventually I decided to say it just once. I said one word and so weakly, you barely responded. Even though I was sitting as far away as possible, I could still see your reaction. I said it again, a little louder, and you obeyed.

"The instant you started to fight, Jordan and Kyle leapt as close to you as they could and started fighting too. They are the reason you lasted as long as you did against us. Both of them fought as hard as they could until they were overtaken. You started to fade, and I told you to stop."

I focus on the part of the story she hasn't mentioned—the most important part. "You made me look at him," I accuse. Did she know I needed to see him one more time?

Clara cocks her head slightly, eyes sad for me. "Whether you want to believe it or not, he did this to you. He was older, smarter, stronger, and very selfish. I made you look at him, because someday you are going to realize the gravity of what he did. You will be glad you watched his final moments, and not out of love for him but for hate."

My heart stops a beat, and I can't decide if I should be terrified of her or not. I want to hate her for talking about Merrick like that, but the hate won't come.

"When will I meet the others?" I ask, brushing her unthinkable prophecy aside.

"I do not know."

"Who decides?"

"I decide, and it is not time yet." Clara stands and I mirror her.

"Please don't go," I plead as she takes a step towards the door. "I can't stop thinking, and I feel like I'm just going in circles in my mind."

"You need to sleep. You are meant to sleep while you are here. You cannot leave this cell until your mind is ready."

"When will that be?"

"Sleep long enough and you will know. If you really need me, I am not far. We will continue the lessons and feedings. When you are ready, I will take you"

I believe her, so I let myself sleep. I let myself dream.

Chapter 11

Angelica

The car ride to my new home travels right through the heart of Chicago. Even though I have seen it all before, it still takes my breath away. Absentmindedly, my hand reaches to rub my neck, sore from staring at skyscrapers too long. The ache reminds me that this isn't real, and I'm not supposed to coast through the memory. I'm here for a reason.

Peter, my new father, drives and hums along to the radio. We are alone and will go the entire ride in silence if I don't speak. Neither of us are talkers, both timid creatures. Nevertheless, I have questions for Peter.

"Are you sure you want me?" I ask.

Peter stops humming. At first, he looks shocked at my question then changes his face quickly into a warm smile.

"Judy and I thought we were being smart on ourselves, having children far apart from each other. Most couples have four or five children, one right after the other. They struggle to make ends meet. But when Vic left for school, Rebecca began to withdraw." Peter sighs, a common reflex when talking about Rebecca. Everyone adores Rebecca, but with Peter it is something more.

He turns the radio up, having spent himself on so many words. Even if he didn't outright answer my question, he said enough. Rebecca chose me at the orphanage, and Peter obliged by bringing me home. In return, I was free of the orphanage and part of a family. But that's not all it cost. If I'd stayed at the orphanage, I wouldn't be in a cell right now.

A chill ghosts through me, like when I confronted Merrick in my dream. *Why did you like me?* I asked him. I will never ask Rebecca that question. Her love is too pure for me to throw back in her face. Instead I reconcile. Staying at the orphanage may not have ended well either, but the idea doesn't stick. There is a hard truth here. Escaping the orphanage, a life with the Franklins, and one blissful year with Merrick weren't worth what I lost.

My body is on autopilot, and by the time my mind catches up, we are already out of the car and walking to the house. Vic is sitting on the steps with Clive and Edison, friends from the neighborhood. Immediately my mood brightens. I'd forgotten this part. In a moment, I'm going to meet Vic, and in him I'll find a new kind of friend. Instead of dark and moody Janice, there will be funny, smart, protective Vic.

The boys on the stairs fall away, and Vic turns to us. He rushes forward to take my suitcase from his dad, and our eyes meet. He's smiling and it makes me smile too. Suddenly I am as shy as I was then. He disappears into the house before I can say a word. Rebecca bounces through the door.

"Angelica!" she squeals and rushes to embrace me. Her touch puts me right again, focuses me on what I want to do.

"I've missed you," I say, letting my arms fall back. It's me talking now, not the memory. When I'm in this place, it's Rebecca that tells me what I need to know. I can't afford to live in the memory when she shows up, no matter how much I want to. Rebecca straightens and looks like she's thinking about whether to go out of character or recite her written lines.

"It hasn't been that long, has it?" Her effortless smile scares me. Is this simply something the real Rebecca would say, my mind knowing her all too well, or is the dream trying to avoid the question? Rebecca has trouble with time, often losing track of the days. If this was really the Franklin's doorstep, I'm not sure she would understand how long it's been. A dark thought crosses my mind. Have these years passed without her understanding I'm never coming back?

I push down the emotion and press on with Rebecca. "I don't want to go in. Can we go for a walk?"

Rebecca wants to say no. It was months before Peter and Judy let us go anywhere without Vic. This version of Rebecca knows that, but it's my dream.

"You know it doesn't matter what we do when we're here, Rebecca. Please." She nods and we start to walk. This memory could change any second, so I must ask the most important thing first.

"How could you let them send me away? They would have done anything for you. Why would you want to be alone again?" The questions spill out on top of each other, accusation heavy in my tone. Everything changed the night they decided to send me away. She looks up at me, frowning.

Rebecca, the street, and the houses all disappear, and when the dream reforms I'm on my bed. Someone is knocking at the door. I sigh because I know exactly what comes next.

"Come in."

A disheveled, unfamiliar Vic sways into my room. I'm nearly seventeen, and my long body takes up most of the bed. Vic manages to find a piece of mattress to sit on. We are about to fight—our only disagreement. Before it starts, I scoot across the bed and lean into him, so I can take in the smell of him one more time. Instead of his clean, fresh scent, he smells sour.

"Don't cry," Vic says, putting his arm around me, lips brushing my cheek. We're ruining the natural order of this memory. He's supposed to tell me about boarding school, and then I laugh in his face. My naïve words are next. I gather my strength and force myself to say my line, but instead of coming out as a confident cackle, it's just a whisper.

"Rebecca will never let me go." My bottom lip quivers, and I cover my face with my hands.

Vic stands, removing his arm from my waist. I hear a crash, then another and another. He's destroying my things, breaking everything into a hundred pieces. This isn't how it really happened, but it's how I feel inside. I watch as he destroys the mementos of a life I'll never touch again. Eventually, I force myself to stand and walk downstairs to take my seat at the table. The memory must continue, and Rebecca is not getting away from me that easily.

By the time I reach the dining room, the family is assembled. Vic sits in his chair, but the crashing sounds from my room continue. No one can hear the destruction but me. When I sit down, I ask Rebecca again.

"Why did you let them send me away?"

"You were failing here," Rebecca says softly. "Everyone knew you were adopted and never let you forget it. You were an outsider." Rebecca would never talk to me like this. They couldn't know what school was like for me. Even so, her words sting with the truth. I glance at Judy and Peter; they are chewing mechanically at their dinner. Rebecca goes on. "If you went away, no one would know anything about you, and you'd get the fresh start you deserved."

"Who told you that, Rebecca? I was doing fine in school!" I scream the lie so loud it pushes me to my feet. "I don't care what they said. I don't care that I didn't have any friends. I had Janice! I had you! I had Vic! I had them!" I gesture to Peter and Judy, who still haven't looked up from their food. "Don't you see? Boarding school was no different to me than the orphanage." I sink back down, exhausted, and reach for her, but her hand slips away.

"You don't really believe that, Rebecca. I know you." Rebecca looks at me and her face, the one I'd know anywhere, is gone. For just a moment, she is unrecognizable. It's a trick to make me doubt myself.

I shut my eyes in frustration, forgetting how tricky this place is, then snap them open in a panic. It's too late, the memory has shifted. It's late and the table is empty. Whispers resonate from another room. After a few seconds, I pick out three distinct voices. I push myself to hear, using my new senses.

"That is not the plan," a man argues, forming his syllables like Clara. A different person tries to speak, but is cut off.

"This is how it is going to be," a woman says, an edge to her voice. She sounds like Judy. I startle and the room goes deathly quiet. "She is awake. Get Rebecca."

I open my eyes to now, to my cell. Immediately I sense someone else and a split second later understand that it's Clara. She is near, but not in the room with me.

"Are you awake now?" she asks from the other side of the cell wall.

"Yes," I whisper back. My voice is raspy and body weak. I have no idea how long I've been asleep, but I'm used to this feeling, the need for blood. The familiar grind of metal on metal follows as Clara comes through the door and sits beside me.

"We have been discussing things." *The three*. Easily I snap back into the now and leave the dream world for the next time I'm alone. "Knowing what you know about cell regeneration and the effects of blood on the Lymerian body, would you like to start feeding from all of us?" Clara's lectures on cell regeneration repeat promptly in my head.

Lymerian cells are affected by everything they encounter. Depending on the source, Lymerian cells can temporarily or permanently change, like the way I was helping Merrick become human. Blood is potent and produces immediate, though often short-lived, changes. It can even influence mood or personality, depending on the will of the Lymerian. Even now, her blood could be shaping me. Clara is making sure to give me small doses so there will be no enduring alterations to my true Lymerian self. Different blood may change nothing, everything, or somewhere in between.

"Will I meet them first?"

"No. It is still too soon. If you choose to add their blood to your diet, I will bring you vials as I normally do."

"What would you do?"

There is a long pause before Clara decides to answer. "I would keep things as they are," she says assuredly. Clara is always so confident.

"Why?" Is she thinking what I'm thinking? Clara opens her mouth to speak then clamps it shut.

"I agreed that I would not persuade you." What kind of deal is that? Why does she bother keeping it in here?

"How would anyone know?"

Clara stands and is beneath a familiar spot on the wall an instant later. I fight to keep my face calm but cannot stop the heat as it flashes across my skin.

"It is time you were told," Clara begins, ignoring my reaction. "We are not far from you. It does take some time to walk at human speeds, and there are twists and turns, but nothing our eyes cannot handle.

"Krisenica was built long after replacement ceremonies started, so it was designed with them in mind. We used to rely on a complex system of mirrors to reflect images from this room to the ones we occupy. But the human invention of cameras changed all that. You are monitored by one of us twenty-four hours a day. They can hear this conversation as well. I will be held completely accountable for anything I say."

This breach of privacy makes me see red, and I say the first thing I think of to hurt her. I want her perfect emotionless mask to drop.

"You already told me your opinion, influenced me. You've broken your word."

"I have not!" Clara moves swiftly, and my feet leave the ground. She's holding me up with her right hand, starring daggers into me. "Do not even think about it, Kyle!" Clara bellows, never taking her eyes off me, then pauses to listen. Her tone sends a shiver down my spine. I stay still, recognizing the miscalculation I made. She's still listening, straining to hear.

I close my eyes, trying to hear what she hears. Clatter, like boxes being knocked over. Fast steps approach and muffled voices. Two different voices getting farther away.

"He cannot help it."

Who is she talking about? Kyle or Jordan?

As if she can read my thoughts, she scoffs. "Kyle." The name takes on a new meaning. Whoever *Kyle* is, he is committed to protecting me. Clara eases me back to the floor.

"What was he trying to do?" I blurt, unable to contain my curiosity.

"Rescue you, I suppose. Things have been going well lately too." She almost frowns, but not quite.

Things have not always gone well? I'm suddenly desperate for more information about these people who have watched me for years.

"What did he think you were going to do?"

"He thought I was going to punish you for questioning my honor. You do not even understand what you said." One way or another, Kyle's attempt to save me from the wrath of Clara did have some effect on the situation.

"I'm sorry, but I don't understand."

"First tell me your answer about the blood, then ask questions."

Of course, I will choose her blood. Reading my thoughts again, Clara pulls a vial from a pocket and hands it to me. It is larger than the others, and I gulp it greedily.

"Slayers are the military of the Lymerians, and I am their commander—their Vegar. It is a great honor and powerful title. If a Lymerian accused me of breaking my word, it would be a serious affront. No one would dare accuse me to my face. One of my captains would handle the offense before it reached my ears." Jealousy twinges in my gut at the fondness in her voice. I avert my focus. Who is in charge of their military while she is away?

"Can you still be in charge of them when you are here?"

"It is unprecedented for someone as high of rank as me to be chosen for Liturgy, so there are no rules regarding it. Let us talk about something else."

Chapter 12

Exams

Written in Jordan's fine hand are the transcriptions from the fourth-year examinations. The Keeper shall be granted access to the transcriptions under the supervision of the Architect.

First visit.

"What is your earliest memory?"

"Hiding in darkness until hands pulled me free. My eyes stayed shut until a nun convinced me to open them at the orphanage."

"How old were you?"

"Four."

"What happened before you were four?"

"I don't know."

"Do you remember your birth parents, your family?"

"No."

Second visit.

"Describe living in the orphanage."

"Many rules and few choices. Janice made it bearable."

"Who is Janice?"

"Another orphan."

"Who is she to you?"

"She was my best friend. My only friend."

"Tell me about her."

"Janice remembered everything. She knew why she was in the orphanage and hated everyone because of it."

"Explain more."

"Janice remembers a baby sister, one she loved more than anything. I wish I could have known the Janice that had a baby sister. The Janice I met didn't have a sister anymore. If my past is anything like Janice's, then I'm glad I can't remember."

Third visit.

"What did you like about the orphanage?"

"Nothing. I liked nothing."

"What did you like about your bedroom at the Franklin's?"

"The tree."

"Why?"

"Because my owl lived there."

"How do you know it was yours?"

"I was the only one that could see it."

"What color was the owl?"

"Many colors mixed together—brown, white, black, gray."

"What did you like about your dorm room?"

"The window."

"Why?"

"It led out. It led to Merrick."

Fourth visit.

"If your house was on fire and you could only save one person, who would that be?"

"Myself."

"You would let the rest die?"

"Peter would save Rebecca. Vic and Judy can take care of themselves."

"Why Peter and not Vic or Judy?"

"Peter . . . I just know he would."

"Explain."

"Rebecca is Peter's responsibility."

"And if Peter were gone?"

"He wouldn't be."

Fifth visit

"Would you rather follow ten rules or one?"

"One."

"Make a rule, and I will follow it."

"Stay near me."

"That is a request, not a rule."

"You must stay near me."

"Impossible, I am Vegar. Amend it."

"No."

"Then I cannot follow it."

Sixth visit.

"What kind of human life did you desire?"

"Marry and raise a family."

"Before you met Merrick, what did you desire?"

"I don't know."

"Yes, you do."

"Before Merrick I thought I'd be with Rebecca and even Vic forever."

Seventh visit.

"Choose three different methods and attack me. Go."

Angelica runs toward Clara and sweeps right arm to the neck. Clara catches the arm, twists then flips Angelica's body into a wall.

On the second attempt, Angelica runs past Clara many times before striking. On the tenth cycle, she spins into the air, kicking her legs out. Clara crouches then springs, gripping Angelica's leg and shoving her into the wall.

"I'll never be able to even scratch you."

"You did before."

Angelica's hand shoots out at Clara's face, touching only air as Clara steps briskly back.

Eighth visit.

"Hold out your hand."

Clara breaks Angelica's pinky finger. Angelica is silent. One by one, Clara breaks the other fingers then feeds her from the wrist.

Ninth visit.

"How long did you live at the orphanage?"

"Nine years."

"Why was Janice your only friend?"

"She didn't like the others."

"You lived at the orphanage for years before Janice. Why did you not have friends?"

"I didn't want them."

"Why?"

"They were weak."

"They were human."

Tenth visit.

"Why did you attack me the first time I came into your cell?"

"Because you smelled like Merrick."

Eleventh visit.

"What was your favorite game when you were human?"

"Chess."

"Who did you play chess with?"

"Vic. He taught me."

"Did you ever beat Vic?"

"I always beat Vic."

"Always? Even in the beginning?"

"Maybe not the first months, but I was learning."

"Why do you think you were so successful against him?"

"Him? I beat everyone in the house, even Peter. Vic never gave up trying to best me. I told him how to win. It's not a race; stop trying to get your king to the other side. Just keep your king alive."

"Did you ever play Rebecca?"

"Rebecca didn't like chess."

Twelfth visit.

"You may ask one question."

"What happened to Janice?"

"Janice is twenty-three. She is not married and has no children. Her life is hard for a human. She makes her meager living by drawing. She still draws you."

Chapter 13

Clara

"She will join us in a few days," I say when I am sure Farrell is done reading the transcripts.

"Has it really been five years?" Farrell sounds bored, but his sharp eyes pay attention to any reaction I might show. "Any other assaults, aside from your original visit?"

"No."

"Did you command her into obedience?" With great effort, I hold back my snicker. May the Astros help the unfortunate Votary beholden to a Litmar Architect.

"I broke her back."

"She marked you?" My ego flares at his lack of surprise.

"Yes." I am torn between pride and shame.

"And her placement?"

"Too soon to determine. Dormant has been eliminated as a possibility."

"I would not say that, Vegar. Your Votary drinks from your blood alone, I presume. You would insist on it. Guard blood will change her, especially the *dijal li* blood. I predict over time she will only be less like you."

"Rude, even for you Farrell." Dijal li blood—imposter's blood. Does he mean Kyle or Jordan?

"Forgive me, I must remember Liturgy has softened you." He pauses to revel in my irritation, aware he is worming his way under my armor. "Jordan, of course, is understandable with your history, but the other? Why should you care for him, Clara? He is but a Dormant hiding in Guard grays." Kyle is the imposter. Only a Litmar would hold a grudge so petty, believing the Astros should not meddle with placement.

There may be truth in what he says, but he is playing a game with me. Litmars love to play games. Pretending Angelica might be a Dormant is his opportunity to needle me about Kyle. Angelica's first examination indicates she is a Guard and Farrell knows it, but odds are she is a Slayer. Votaries usually follow the same division as their Architect or become Dormants. Her behavior has only once suggested she is Slayer, but she is certainly not a Dormant. The real exams are to come, and the Council has the final say.

"We would like to review the scrolls," I say, changing the subject. I am done playing his game. Farrell nods, satisfied, and picks up the phone receiver closest to him. He does not speak into it. Instead he dials a combination of numbers with intermittent pauses. I can hear the beeping responses through the receiver but have no idea what the codes mean.

Farrell hangs up the phone. "Someone will meet you at Mountain Top."

Before I can stop myself, my heart and breathing pause from the shock of what he has said. Farrell can no doubt hear my body's reaction to the news. *Mountain Top.*

"How many times have you met with the Astros?"

Farrell knows how many times I have been called. "Twice."

Visits to the Astros are calculated and rare. Younger Lymerians have only seen Etherial, the Astro that resides on the High Council. In my earlier years, it was different. Lymerians were invited to council meetings and sometimes small groups of Astros would be there too.

Occasionally Lymerians are called into Astros quarters, yet no one speaks of it. Astros cover their tracks, clearing all memory of your encounter. As Vegar, I have been called to Mountain Top twice. There is very little I recall of either visit.

"You must have known they would meet with you, as Architect."

"Perhaps not so soon," I offer honestly.

"They follow no rules." Farrell is correct. Older and more experienced than I, he speaks the truth of them. They follow no rules and hold all power. Yet we submit; we trust. I trust them.

We nod to each other, and I leave.

* * *

Krisenica is isolated within the Appalachian Mountains to keep it hidden from humans. Lymerians arrived with the first European settlers. Dormant builders spent decades carving the mountain so it would be habitable for the rest that eventually followed. Over the years, we have added and updated, making it into a grand facility. A mere mountain on the outside, but our world away from a world inside.

Angelica, Kyle, Jordan, and I reside at the lowest point, which is hundreds of feet below ground. Most of Krisenica weaves through the mountains. The Astros live at Mountain Top, the most secure place in Krisenica.

Thankfully there is an elevator that travels some of the distance. Inside it awaits a single coat, a pair of boots, and thick gloves. For a moment, I think about not taking them, but the memory of my last encounter with this mountain tells me different. Near the top of the mountain there is snow and fast winds, and the entrance at the top is hidden.

When I step out of the elevator, I look to the south. Nadir is not far. Thinking of him and our remote days spent in Africa fill me with warmth. I will need to hold on to this feeling as I climb.

"*Njoo Kwangu,*" I whisper, letting the wind carry my message to its destination, and then I start moving.

There are many miles to climb, but with my speed, distance passes quickly. When I come upon the place where the entrance once lived, I find it changed. It does not surprise me. Nothing is ever easy with the Astros. Whether it is for their protection, entertainment, or reasons I cannot begin to imagine, there is no entrance here. I must find a different way.

Another frigid hour goes by before I spot a break in the mountainside. Only Lymerian eyes could see the faint glow breaking free of rock. As I approach, I feel small vibrations and hear humming. It is familiar, and I remember everything they made me leave behind during the last visit. Those memories were not taken nor erased, simply locked away, and only they have the key. How will I hold on to them? What if I ran right now? Before I can decide, the mountain parts. With a burst of speed, I slide in before it closes.

Blackness—not even my eyes can see. Quickly I reach for a wall and feel around until I touch what I need. The room illuminates to reveal an Astro I know as Carmen standing very near me. Her eyes are blindingly white.

"To see what you see," I say in amazement and everything goes black again.

It is night when I find myself back at the entrance to the elevator. There is no sign of Nadir, but he feels near. A game of hide and seek. I shut my eyes and concentrate until I see myself through his. When I turn to where he should be, there is only snow and mountain.

"Nadir you win," I say, and he moves a little. Ah, his color is different. We move as one and collide together. "You are so beautiful. Do you like the snow?" Nadir licks my face, his happiness pulsing through us both.

Nadir is my compeer. We have been together since Africa, since I was a child. Any Lymerian has the ability to choose a compeer, but it is only the Slayers and Guards that see the use in having them.

Nadir is a black panther, and his blood intensifies my power, speed, agility, and many senses. In return, he shall live as long as I do and may live wherever he chooses. Centuries of my blood allow him to adapt to his surroundings. His fur is white from the years living in the mountains and snow. Despite our link, he remains fiercely independent. Throughout our many lifetimes, he is away as much as with me.

His loyalty took years to earn and required a great risk. For an entire year I followed him through the jungles of Africa, abandoning the Lymerians and my Slayer training. I knew from the first time I saw him that he was worth it. I would not have risen to Vegar without him. When the Lymerians set sail across the Atlantic, Nadir followed me.

Since we have been in America, he spends most of his time in the South American jungles. Two decades ago he came back to Krisenica and has been living in the mountains ever since. This is our fourth meeting in that time and the first I have seen him white.

"You are going to lose this beautiful coat," I tease and rub the side of my face against his. He licks me again, whispering such sadness into my I heart that I pull away. Then I fix my gaze on him and let his thoughts envelope me.

Lymerians and compeers can communicate with each other, better over time. Nadir knows my words, especially Swahili, but his English is coming along. Animal communication is different. They think single thoughts over and over until they are acknowledged. They may think *happy, happy, happy* as they greet you or *love, love, love* when they rub their face against your hands. Right now, Nadir is thinking *leave, leave, leave.* He is ready to leave again. The jungle is calling him, and he wants me to go too.

I smile just a little at his love for me, and a single tear escapes me. Angelica will not leave Krisenica for many years. Nadir lays across my lap and stretches his neck. He wants to show me something. I remove my creese—a small, sharp sword—and slide it across the side of Nadir's neck, swallowing twice from him.

My mind floods with images of Nadir and I running through the jungles of Africa. Adventure, hunting, hills, the burning sun, cool water—my truest happiness. In his mind, we are forever young and strong. More memories, ones where we are not alone. Nadir knows and is trying to help me. I hold him close, feeling the end nearing us.

"Have you lived enough lives, my friend?" Without my blood, he will live one final lifetime. "Do you wish to join her?" Nadir's mind is quiet. Undecided. "For now then?" Once again, I remove the creese and slash it across my wrist. Nadir licks and his beautiful green eyes turn black, as does his white coat. He is a panther again. My blood gives him more than my dark eyes. It tells him why I cannot leave.

Nadir stands and licks my face one last time. We look into each other's eyes for a long time before he thinks *her, her, her, stay, stay, stay, kwaheri, kwaheri, kwaheri.*

Chapter 14

Clara

Kyle is on watch in the viewing room when I finally make my way back down to our quarters. I stop by to check in. Kyle stands, assuming I am here to relieve him, but when his eyes meet mine he sits back down. Seeing through my mask, he knows I cannot take my watch right now.

Despite lifetimes of cultivating the art of masking my own feelings, Jordan and Kyle see through me. There is no Slayer. There is no Vegar. *Nothing shall come between the three, and they shall see, see, see.* Liturgy wins every time. Their transparency is equal to mine—a small comfort. Kyle does not mind a second watch; he is probably delighted to have more time observing Angelica.

Instead of seeking my room, I go to Jordan. Much of my clothes are wrecked from the cold and climb, so I remove them and slide in his bed. Since my breakdown, I have given in to my need for Jordan. It is not the passion of our youth, but layers of protection, loyalty, and love.

"You saw Nadir?" Jordan asks, surprised. "How long has he been here? I thought he was in the Amazon."

"He returned in 1939." Jordan sucks in a breath. The year my mate left.

"Nadir knew you needed him." I nod. "He has gone back then?"

"Why do you think that?"

"You are incredibly sad. Did you tell him about your Guards and Angelica?"

"Yes."

"And he still left?"

"Nadir yearns for the days of our youth."

"Nadir is right. Forgive me, Clara . . ." Jordan lets my hair loose and looks deep into my eyes. "When you returned with Nadir, there was a light within the blackness of your eyes. I still dream of it." He does not speak of the years that followed, and his suffering as he watched, helpless, while the light burned out. Regret is written all over him, from the downcast stare to his slumping shoulders and shallow breaths.

"He meant for me to return to the Amazon with him. Now, he may never come back." I return us to the now, unwilling to remember Africa's many treasures and the travesties they endured when we left.

Jordan's arms tighten around me. "It is for the best. He has been your compeer far longer than any of our other compeers." It hurts to hear him say that, but he is right. "Your eyes are absolutely stunning though. I will miss that." Jordan goes quiet, and my eyelids grow heavy. Just as I am on the brink of sleep, he says, "Could do without the panther smell."

I smile faintly and sleep.

* * *

The next morning, we meet in the viewing room. Angelica is ready to join us, and there is much to discuss. Kyle speaks first.

"What did Farrell say about the exams?"

"Little. He advises us to keep all divisions in mind."

"And the scrolls?" Jordan asks. His question sparks a familiar buzz, Astro tinged. Everything beyond the break in the mountain is a blur of disconnected images. The buzzing intensifies until a memory slips back in place. This is how it works with Astros. Your memories come back when you reach the correct marker. Jordan has triggered a marker.

"Farrell sent me to Mountain Top. The scrolls will be here soon." Jordan and Kyle stare at me, astonished. "Do not try to push information out of me. You know how it works." Disappointed, they sink down into their seats.

"That is good," Jordan says, taking control of the conversation again. "Clara exchanged with Nadir last night—Angelica must feed from us. Once we meet, she should be receptive to new blood."

"Since you and Kyle are guards, you can take turns." I pause noticing Kyle's red face and pursed lips forming an ill-fitting expression.

"You cannot be the only one to feed her, Kyle. Especially at your age," Jordan says gently. Kyle nods a few times, trying to shake his unease. Sharing blood is intimate, and Jordan is a male Guard. Even Liturgy cannot quell this Lymerian instinct.

"Kyle, I wish you could understand . . ." Jordan shakes his head. "Here, I will show you." Jordan pulls his own creese from his side and swipes his wrist before Kyle can argue. I have already given Jordan a vial, and a moment later Kyle is drinking. "Could you see enough?"

Kyle softens and nods.

Jordan cannot show Kyle images as I can show Nadir, but Jordan's blood is his essence. When Lymerians drink another's blood, they understand them better. It is easier to discern lies from truths. Rarely do we share our blood.

"Moving on," I say. "We will barricade the elevator tomorrow. Someone must get Kyle's final stock of blood today." They look at each other, weighing who has the worse plight. Kyle has not been to the surface in five years, unwilling to part from Angelica. Jordan has not returned since the night I fell apart, avoiding Karina. I nod to Jordan and he exhales. He will go to the surface for the blood and to end centuries of partnership.

"Jordan, you will need to gather supplies for the barricade. This room gets locked as well. No doubt she could pry her way in if she wished, but let us hope she ignores the room. While we are thinking of rooms, is hers ready?"

Kyle nods. They were working on that yesterday.

"When all is done, we get her."

Chapter 15

Angelica

Clara says it's been five years since I came here with Merrick. It never occurred to me to keep track of time in Krisenica. The three agonizing days I spent in this room as a human are still vivid in my memory. If someone told me then that this would be my home for five years, I would have gone mad before becoming one of them.

Now that I am one of them, time doesn't scare me. Part of me still misses Rebecca and Vic and Janice, but I can contain the sadness. I have come to realize that they will be fine. Vic and Rebecca have each other. Janice has herself—the only person she ever really needed. My company was an improvement on their lives, but not a necessity. Here, I must focus on myself and this future. At least that's what I tell myself every day.

They are coming, my inner voice whispers. The voice that used to beg me to remember my humanity has changed allegiances. It accepts who I am now, letting go of my human life. Hundreds of years from now, will my human years feel like a dream or will they be this clear forever?

Three—it is three this time. There are never three.

I shake off the warning and move to the door, ready for who is coming.

"It is time," Clara announces after she thrusts open the door for the final time. On either side of her stand two men, both well over six feet tall. They look like they could run through a wall. Most importantly, they are the human kind of Lymerian. Too familiar is this moment to the last time I left this cell. Matching Guards escorting me to a new life. Unease forms in the pit of my stomach. I try to ignore it.

At first glance, they look very similar. Identical gray uniforms, standing with feet shoulder width apart, arms clasped behind backs, same haircut and same height. When I look closer, the pale, fair haired one has a softness to him, kind eyes, and round cheeks. The other is stern with dark hair and olive skin.

"He is your Guard?" I ask Clara, gesturing to the dark one. Clara doesn't answer. She doesn't even move a muscle. "You don't need a Guard," I add, irritated by her silence and by something else I can't quite put into words.

Silently, I question everything. Is Liturgy a fancy word for kidnapping, corrupting, and assimilating? Anger creeps from my depths, begging to be let free. My inner voice prepares me for the worst. Everyone goes still. For several minutes, no one moves or speaks. Are they thinking about throwing me back in that cell? I won't let them.

"Angelica," the pale Guard breaks the silence, and I turn to him, relieved. Our eyes lock and electricity glides across my skin. The connection is instant. Everything Clara has told me is true. My heart starts beating faster until I realize they can hear this proof of my panic. I fight to calm down, but it's no good. Years of memories flood me. Hundreds of faces, thousands of eyes that held nothing for me. Yet in this Lymerian, there is everything: safety, love, honor, and friendship.

"Calm down," Clara says and everything inside me goes still. "Meet Kyle and Jordan."

"You didn't have to do that," I say, ignoring the Guards. Clara has not done that since just after my year without blood.

"Yes I did. There is nothing more dangerous than a Votary, which is why their Architect can influence their actions to a certain extent. Of course, it all depends on the will of the Architect."

"Lucky for me I got the most stubborn Architect that ever was." I can't help but sneer a little as I say it. Kyle chuckles, but I don't look, fearful of how I might react.

"Angelica, there is a reason you are kept away from everyone. This will not be easy, and Lymerians will not accept you until you prove yourself. That could take decades. Meanwhile, you have three friends in this world. Three that will do anything to protect you. We may not be what you expected, but I promise we are the best for you. We will go when you are ready—not when you say you are ready, but when we know that you are ready."

Kyle looks at Clara. "Why is she reacting like this?"

"I'm right here, Kyle," I say, still not looking at him. Clara rolls her eyes and glares at Kyle.

"Who remembers the way Angelica reacted the first time she met me?" Clara pauses, letting the memory of that day settle over us. "This is a process, Kyle, remember?" All her arrogance and flare is gone, revealing a hidden softness, another layer to Clara.

Even though I am sick of this cell, part of me wants to plant my feet and grip the door. It is safe, familiar, and all mine. Another part of me wants to run like hell from this cell to whatever fate is out there for me.

"Is this who I am, Clara? Is this the kind of Lymerian I'm going to be?"

"It is hard to know the nature of a Votary. You have had Slayer blood in your veins for years and soon you will accept a Guard's blood." Before my body can announce my anxiety at taking in new blood, I squash it. I don't want them to know. "I did not know you before, so I cannot say how it will all turn out," she finishes.

"Yes," Kyle says softly. "Votaries are equally matched with their Architects. You already remind me very much of Clara. Believe me, after spending years in the same room with her, I know her some."

My eyes shift to Jordan, silently asking his thoughts.

"Kyle and I are ordinary Guards despite Clara's testimony. At least we were ordinary—now we are more. Nothing is ever for certain, Angelica. When you live as many lifetimes as we have, you learn that." He nods at me. "Time to go now. We are wasting time."

Jordan turns, followed by Clara, then me with Kyle last in line. As Kyle steps into his place, I feel the charge again, the connectedness to something meant to be.

Everything down here looks the same, like one big cell. The walls are carved out of the same part of the mountain and given smooth edges. The air remains stagnant. I'd hoped we would gain elevation, but the way is flat. Jordan and Kyle are tense in comparison to Clara's casual stride. Is this what all Guards are like? Jordan finally stops when we reach four doorways.

"These are our rooms. Yours is next to Clara's, across from Kyle's." Jordan gestures to one of the doorways.

"No doors?" I ask.

The three of them exchange looks.

"Krisenica has few doors," Clara offers eventually.

I glance down the hallway. It's far, but there is a way out. Blocked. Seeing another locked door invites my anger back.

Clara misses nothing. "Time will pass quickly. When you are ready, we will go upstairs together."

Together is the only thing I hear. From now on, we are together. I feel the anger pull back. "What's next then?" I ask, perhaps for the first time understanding that everything is different now. Clara cannot announce the beginning and end of a lesson by breezing in and out of my cell. We will be together all the time. My stomach sinks. Rows of girls flicker in my mind as I remember the orphanage, then the dorms—living arrangements I despised. There will be no privacy, not even the illusion of privacy I had in the cell.

Before anyone can answer, I disappear into my door-less room. It is empty except for a bed, nightstand, and small light. A bed is an improvement I suppose. The others separate into their own rooms. Every step, shift, and sigh bounces off walls and grinds on my ears. From now on, this is how it will be. Upstairs, even worse until I can learn to live with all the noise.

I lie down and focus on the future. Clara promised we would live together and so we are. Which means her second promise is also true. We will go upstairs together someday. Then what? I become part of a race of beings living in secret, forever confined inside Krisenica.

There is still enough human inside of me to rebuke this future. I reach for the little light, and let sleep come.

The next time my eyes open, Vic is sitting in the corner of my room. Though my dreams have decreased over time, this is the first one that isn't in a memory. We are definitely beneath Krisenica.

Without a memory to create the rules, Vic looks different. His features are sharper and more pronounced. My brain must be trying to make Vic look older, to age him with the years that have gone by. I've made his hair grow out straight and match the soft shade of his brown eyes. Even his clothes are different—he's in black. Do I think he is mourning me?

"Angelica," Vic whispers. I start to sit up, not wanting to waste any time with dream Vic. But before I can get far, he is by my side with his arms on top of mine. Very slowly he leans into me, lips parted slightly as he kisses the top of my head. A sound outside the door pulls him away from me. "Do not tell them you saw me."

Vic is gone and Kyle is in the doorway.

"How long have you been there?" I ask, sitting up.

"I heard you moving around and . . ." He shrugs.

"So you are my Guard, in charge of keeping me safe no matter what?"

Kyle nods. "It's more than just that, though. Clara and I work together as you transition into Lymerian society. We balance each other out by bringing two completely different interests to the table, though both of us are devoted to you." I steal a glance and take in his flushed face.

"I didn't think Lymerians had much of an emotional range," I say, just a hint of a teasing in my voice. "Well, at least not like humans." I sound like me when I'm talking to Kyle. If I close my eyes, it could be me teasing Vic in my room with Rebecca playing nearby.

"I'm not your ordinary Lymerian. I tell jokes too." He smiles, making him less like a gray hooded Guard, and more like . . . Kyle.

I decide to risk meeting his eyes again. They are inviting bright blue orbs that put me at ease. The electricity I felt before is now a dull drum, content to thud quietly between our beating hearts. Kyle either doesn't notice or isn't surprised by the sensation. He prattles on without missing a beat.

"Honestly, I probably could have fit well into a Dormant life. Dormants tend to either have a genuine emotional range or are able to copy humans." Kyle crosses the room and sits at the end of the bed. "Actually, I'm pretty sure the Council intended to place me as a Dormant, but Etherial spoke Guard for me."

"Who is Etherial?"

"Part of the Council, the Astro, in fact." Clara never named anyone specifically on the council. I lean in, waiting for more.

"Clara has spoken of government to you before, but we can look at it closer if you want." I nod. "Litmars are the smallest division and do day-to-day governing. They work together with the High Council, also known as the Council. The Council is called on for really important matters, but may intercede at any level of government. There are eight on the council: Anubis, a Slayer; Etherial, an Astro; Valencia, a Dormant; Reina, a Litmar; and the *Téssera*, their Guards. The four Guards are each assigned to one of the non-Guard council members and together have one vote. Etherial only votes when there is a tie between the others or when a ruling of the Council would alter the trajectory of our existence." Kyle stops so I can take in everything.

I nod to show that I'm following. "Why is the opinion of an Astro so important?"

"It is not just one Astro," Clara says from the doorway, and both Kyle and I involuntarily jerk. "Etherial is connected to all of them. Etherial's vote is that of all the Astros," Kyle looks upset, but Clara wears the hint of a smile on her face. "Do not take it so hard, Kyle. You are Guard and I am Vegar. I can sneak up on anyone."

Kyle turns away from me to stare at the wall. I try to wrap my head around what Kyle's placement means.

"What you're saying is that the Astros interfered with your placement. You had to be a Guard . . . my Guard and part of Liturgy. Which means the Astros saw this, all of this. How old are you?" My head is spinning from trying to understand. Merrick meeting me seemed so random. Clara was right. Astros are much more than psychics.

"Angelica, no one understands the Astros, except perhaps other Astros. I have been trying to understand them for centuries and have not gotten far." Clara glances to Kyle before changing subjects. "We thought you should feed."

Kyle reaches into one of his belt pockets and pulls out a small sword. I've seen Clara with one of those before. At first I don't get it, but when I do my heart beat picks up. "Why not a vial?"

"Well, I just thought . . . a vial is so formal. We used it in the beginning so it would be more human for you. We don't carry them around or anything. Most of us feed so infrequently that it doesn't really make sense to bother with a vial." Kyle is rambling, possibly lying, so I save him from himself by asking a question.

"How will I know when to stop?" What if I can't stop? Sweet blood is energy and strength but always measured.

"Just a few sips," Clara says, with her classic confidence. At least one of us is sure I can stop. "Kyle holds a creese. It is quite sharp and can cut very deep if you are not careful. Kyle will make the cut and then you sip."

He does it swiftly, and I eagerly pull his wrist to my mouth, taking two sips. It's different than Clara's, not so bold. I have to fight the temptation to let my shoulders slack. He is naturally more relaxed than either Clara or me.

"Where's Jordan?"

"Sleeping. We've been rotating sleeping shifts for years," Kyle says.

"Guards need a lot of sleep too," Clara points out and Kyle gives her a look, but it's friendly. He's forgiven her for sneaking up on us earlier. They are more to each other than I first realized. So much like siblings. *Vic,* my inner voice reminds me and the urge to be alone swallows me.

"Can I lie back down?" The last thing I want is to lie down, but it's an excuse to be alone. Clara and Kyle nod and leave. I stare across the room, wishing for Vic. We were never quite brother and sister, more like cherished friends.

Reality strikes me in the chest. I will never see the real Vic again. Memories and dreams is all there is, forever. One day I won't distinguish the dreams from the true reality.

"Vic," I whisper. Very tired suddenly, I slip down to lying but keep my eyes fixed. Tears leak down the edge of my nose. "I miss you."

Chapter 16

Clara

"Sleep," I say a third time before Angelica closes her eyes. "One dose of your blood and she is a wreck." Kyle and I walk to Jordan's room and pick out chairs.

"Emotions are okay now. She has us to support her. She's not alone in a room day after day." Kyle is bubbling with happiness. It is a bit nauseating to see him like this. "She can't hide from her feelings forever. This time down here, together, is supposed to be about moving past human experiences and emotions with a support system." I roll my eyes.

"You are such a Dormant," Jordan says to Kyle as he sits up from sleep. "Can the two of you debate without waking me up?" Kyle and I look at each other, confused.

"Sorry, habit," I say quickly. "We normally talk in the viewing room and . . ." I trail off.

"That's blocked," Kyle offers.

"And we were not going into my room," I add.

"Nor mine."

Jordan waves at Kyle to stop talking and shakes his head. "Once again, I am the only one here that can think clearly. We have had her out mere hours, and you already put her to sleep I gather?" I nod yes. "You cannot do that every time you want to talk about her. The time for analyzing Angelica has passed. You had five years for that. It is time to move forward with the process."

"It's not as easy as it sounds. We have to teach her everything about our kind and get her to open up. Her next exams determine placement," Kyle says in our defense.

"Which is why the process takes years. Are you finally getting what Clara has been trying to show you all this time? It cannot happen overnight. She is nowhere near the Lymerian she will be someday. Right now she is still so human."

Jordan's words settle on us. They are disappointing to hear, but he is right. The years already spent with Angelica were simply to ensure that she would not be a threat to anyone, that she had physically transitioned.

"Her mind and body have healed, but her heart is another thing entirely. We have to win her over." Jordan looks at me then Kyle. "You two have to win her over."

"Why didn't you say this yesterday?" Kyle asks with a dramatic eye roll, lightening the serious tone in the air. Jordan is not amused.

"When she wakes, we begin. We have to teach her about Lymerians as a whole and specifically about ourselves," I say, also ignoring Kyle's joke. "From now on we use the cell if we want to talk. It is far enough away that she will not be able to hear us."

"How are you going to teach her about *your* history?" Kyle asks.

"I will tell her everything when she is ready."

"That isn't an answer. Last time you decided when she was ready, we were all wrecked for weeks. Here's what we should do. I focus on late Norse to now. You two are from the same surge—Jordan can cover Africa and early Norse. Clara, anything pre-Africa is your responsibility."

The Vegar in me does not want to follow a plan that is not mine, but Kyle's idea makes sense.

"It is a good plan, Kyle," Jordan says, rescuing me from admitting Kyle's plan is better than mine.

"Okay," I say finally, and we begin.

* * *

Over the next several months, we become teachers, each with a different specialty. Jordan spends his time with Angelica talking about our glory days in Afri-terra, or Africa as it is now called. He makes sure to include personal details about both of our experiences. Just as Kyle suggested, it makes sense that Jordan speak for us both.

This arrangement works very well, and I see a new relationship forming. He is the father Angelica always yearned for, and Jordan has found his place in Liturgy. They are never affectionate, not like human father and daughter, but he affects her. When Jordan is around, Angelica straightens. When he speaks, she hangs on his words. When he compliments her training, I see the smile in her eyes.

As one might expect, Angelica quickly warms to Kyle's good nature. His adoration is in every word, gesture, and glance. He would do anything for her—would die for her. It is unlikely anyone has ever cared for her that deeply. When they are together, they sit a little too close and let their arms graze against each other. Twice I see her embrace him. Perhaps I should not credit everything to Liturgy; Kyle is very likeable. He puts people at ease and makes them laugh.

My fears about Kyle being left to his own devices with Angelica lessen, though do not disappear entirely. He is a devoted friend to her, and she has accepted his friendship. Our hope is that she will trust him with secrets from her human life. Secrets we can use to determine her placement and monitor progress.

But even after months together, their conversations continue to focus on Kyle. She does not mention Merrick, and I wonder how much she is holding on to. They were together for a year and more than six have passed since his death. How can we know if it is behind her?

It is my job to break Angelica out of the mindset of a human. Her new body, forged by the blood of the Council elders, has capabilities beyond her wildest fantasies. There are significant training limitations down here, but we make the best of it. When she breaks free of the human mindset, she will understand her potential.

After a year of training together, she is not extraordinary. Not once have I sensed the dangerous Angelica who fought through the crowd during the ceremony or the savage girl that attacked me again and again without fear. Nevertheless, I train her as I would one of my Slayers. No matter what future Liturgy holds, she was given the Vegar as Architect for a reason. One way or another, I will find what is hiding within her.

* * *

"If I run that fast, I'm going to go straight into a wall."

Angelica and I have been arguing about this for weeks. She is to run to her old cell and back while I time her. Then run again and beat the previous time. It is a simple task.

"You are talking like a Dormant," I say, more than a little irritated.

"Maybe I am a Dormant," Angelica says defiantly. Jordan's scoff reaches us from down the hall. We make eye contact. My eyes blaze triumph while hers stay obstinate. "Of *course* Jordan is going to agree with you."

"Should we have the conversation again? Everyone agrees that you are not a Dormant. You did not even like humans when you were one. Name one friend that you had." Before she can speak, I add, "Not Janice—she was barely human." I say it as a compliment and Angelica knows it. From the little I have been told of Janice, I feel I would like her. Angelica crosses her arms, unwilling to dignify my question with an answer.

"Whatever division you are, it has been with you always. You never wanted to be in that world. You tolerated it. You did not care about the future. You did not care about school and did not fit in" Angelica drops her arms and stands up straight, getting ready to make an argument. I do not let her. "Plans with Merrick do not count."

"Why doesn't it count?" Angelica's passionate response dwindles before she can complete the sentence. I glare at her, half warning and half daring her to push me.

"Kyle, I can hear you inching closer to us. You are not coming to her rescue. It is my session." Faintly, I hear his footsteps retreat, then Jordan's hushed voice. The two of them are sucking up my last bit of patience. Instead of having an outburst, I breathe. "Plans made with a loved one, especially at the beginning of a relationship, are based on the desire to spend time together." Angelica stares at me. "It means you really liked him," I say flatly. "It does not mean you planned a future." She does not reply. Perhaps I should not have mentioned Merrick. But we need to stop tiptoeing around it. I try again.

"Skills are developed based on the body's needs. You will not be able to hear miles away until you convince your body it needs to. You will not be able to outrun a car until you have shown your body how to. Our cells will regenerate and adapt to whatever circumstance this planet has to offer. It will be painful, but that is how we earn our talents and skills."

"What if I don't care about this place either?" she asks stubbornly.

"Litmars make our laws and monitor the economics and politics of all the countries on Earth. Dormants are our eyes and ears of the everyday human. They learn invaluable trades and services from being part of the human world. Guards save lives, both human and Lymerian. Slayers win wars and conquer darkness, both human and Lymerian. Can you find something in there to care about?"

Angelica stands up straight, as if she has finally heard something that makes sense to her. "And the pain?" I have almost convinced her.

"Eventually you stop noticing the pain," I say. "Run as fast as you can to the cell and back."

Chapter 17

Angelica

It's been over a year since I left my cell, but we visit it often as a training site. Gouges decorate the walls and floors, some there on purpose and others . . . accidents. Clara uses every part of the dungeons to train me, always coming up with something new and never running out solutions to problems.

Being able to heal fast drives the Lymerians to push and work harder than a human ever could. There are no limits to what Clara will ask me to do, because she knows that I can heal from any sort of injury I incur. There have been countless broken bones, gashes, constant scabs and bruises. Everything she wants me to do hurts. Sometimes I must feed from all three of them to heal. If I'm really upset with the session, I'll refuse their blood and wait for my body to heal on its own. Jordan and Kyle don't like it when I do that, but I think it makes Clara happy. She wants me to be tough, to work through my discomfort.

Kyle says born Lymerians train for decades before they are given a division, while a Votary has about ten years to prepare. Liturgy allows more to be accomplished in less time.

Fun fact. Newborn Lymerians are considered children for their first hundred years on Earth. Physically they are fully grown after thirty human years. Since a Lymerian body changes based on what it takes in, aging the body is easy.

Clara is pushing my body to the limits, but I'm the only one that can push my brain. I'm obsessed with remembering every detail of every day. Each morning I play out my life since the moment I woke up in the cell and knew I was one of them. Between the long periods of sleep and moments lost in memories, the beginning years are not as precise as recent ones.

"Good timing," I say, hearing Jordan as I finish the memory exercise. "How do you know when I'm ready each morning?"

"Your breathing changes," Jordan says bluntly and sits down in the chair next to my bed. The chair used to be in Jordan's room, but he moved it in here for lessons. Jordan takes out his creese. "How are feeling? Clara says you refused to feed yesterday. Has everything healed?" I nod. I'm healing faster and faster every day. "You better feed anyway. You need to keep up your strength."

Any time I'm being stubborn and Clara and Kyle want me to feed, they send in Jordan. They know I won't turn him away. Jordan slices across his arm, and I sip from him. The blood scatters inside of me, soothing places I didn't even realize needed attention.

"Don't tell Kyle, but I think I like your blood the best," I say, watching his skin heal. For just a few minutes after each feeding with Jordan, I am my old human self. Memories so real overpower me, like sunshine on my face or the smell of fresh cut grass. Hard to believe it's been six years down here. At least I'm not the only one stuck here, I guess.

"He can probably hear you," Jordan replies in his firm, all-business tone. I wish Kyle were here, if only to ease Jordan's tension. Kyle even gets Jordan to laugh sometimes. His jokes are usually at Clara's expense, so Jordan's deep chuckle is always short lived. I can't help wanting to hear Jordan let go in a hearty belly laugh.

Kyle and Clara bicker like brother and sister, and I am their favorite toy they must share. Clara always wins though, because Kyle backs down. For a second, I try to imagine Kyle standing his ground, fighting Clara.

"What are you smiling at?" Jordan interrupts.

"I was trying to imagine what a real fight would look like between Clara and Kyle." Before Jordan can stop himself, he flashes a smile.

For one brief moment, I see his teeth. "What? Tell me. For goodness sake, Kyle can't hear us. Neither can Clara for that matter. Both of them are in the cell."

"How do you know that?" Jordan asks, surprised.

"I can always sense when they are near. In my cell, I sometimes felt like Clara was gone entirely." Jordan nods. "The sensation was dull then. When I met Kyle, I really felt it, the electric pulse. Since then I've been keeping an eye it, noticing when it's strong or weak."

"Tracking," Jordan confirms. "Possibly a side effect of Liturgy or an indication of something more." I wait, hoping he is going to explain what that means. "The skill can be used by both Guards and Slayers. Slayers use tracking to hunt people. Guards use it as a lifeline between themselves and their ward. Very skilled Guards can reach for anyone with their tracking sense."

"Lifeline . . . so like to know where they are?"

"Exactly, like what you just did with Clara and Kyle. But that could also be Liturgy connecting you to them." I nod, understanding he doesn't want to take a side. Clara is team Slayer and Kyle is team Guard. Still, I might be neither.

"What about tracking other people?" I ask, firing off another question. "Why would a Guard do that?"

"To know how they are feeling, if they are lying. The stronger your emotional connection to the other Lymerian, the more accurate the sense." Guards are sneaky. A silence follows as I realize Jordan knew where Clara was this whole time; Kyle too. Was he just testing me?

"Keep tracking them," Jordan instructs, then smiles. "If you promise not to bring it up around them, I will tell you about the time Kyle tried—" He smiles again and looks down. "I am sorry, it really is quite funny looking back. The time he tried to fight Clara."

"What?!" I exclaim, nearly forgetting everything he just said. "I thought she was unbeatable. How could a Guard possibly stand a chance?"

"He thought I was going to fight with him." My jaw drops.

"You'd never hurt Clara. Didn't he understand that?"

Jordan shakes his head. "It was in the beginning, before we understood how the three of us fit together."

"So what happened?" I'm on the edge of my bed now, buzzing with excitement. A near forgotten delight tickles my heart—fun.

"Well . . ." Jordan begins.

"You are not backing out. Please, please, please."

Jordan sighs. "They are both going to be upset. Pay attention to your tracking. As soon as you know they are headed back, stop me." I nod, folding my feet under me and sitting straight up.

"Kyle was not himself at the beginning. It took him years to relax and be as you know him now. At first, he was tense and very worried about you. If you are truly a Guard, someday you will understand how unbearable it was for him to see you suffering. His first instinct was to challenge the person that stood in the way of himself and his ward."

Jordan pauses, and it reminds me of the last time someone told me a story. Vic used to tell Rebecca and me stories, battle stories from history—his favorite subject. He liked to dramatically pause and keep us on the edge of our seats before going on. That same anticipation hangs between us.

"Kyle assumed that the two Guards chosen for Liturgy were to balance out the power of the Architect, but he had it all wrong. Before anyone could explain that to him, he pushed Clara too far, which as you know does not take much.

"I hope you can see her in her true form someday," Jordan adds. "Right now, she is not the Vegar. She is your Architect. That constant fire that burns inside her has dwindled here. Make no mistake, she is the deadliest person in the world. When we go upstairs, she will be that person again."

I go cold because I know he is telling the truth. "Kyle picked a fight with the deadliest person in the world?" Jordan nods. "For me?" Affection for Kyle warms away the cold. Kyle hasn't tried to hide his feelings for me, but this is the first time I've heard of him acting on them. I refocus. "What happened next?"

"It was over in seconds. Clara delivered three blows with a chair then nearly suffocated him."

My jaw drops. "How did you get her to stop?"

"I asked her," Jordan says softly. "Kyle held it against me for some time, that I had not sided with him. But eventually he could see the way he feels about you is exactly how I feel about Clara, and there is nothing either of us can do about it."

Would Jordan trade places with another if he could? Does he resent the control he's under?

"You know how he feels, right?" I nod gently. "You do not have to feel the same way. The last thing you need is a mate. Find out who you are first."

I think about that. Being around Kyle isn't like being around Merrick, but I like it when he stands close or touches me accidentally. He is strong and devoted, and if I ask him to stay he will never leave me. Would I want to live forever simply being content, and never feel the fire in my heart that I felt with Merrick?

"Forever is a long time," Jordan says, reading my mind. "You never know who will come into your life."

"You can't leave a mate?"

Jordan looks down for a long time before he answers. "You can, but at great cost. Our bonds are meant to last centuries, much longer than a human lifetime. When they break, it is a much deeper anguish than a human can comprehend." I may not be able to sense Jordan the way I can Kyle and Clara, but I'm sure Jordan left his mate for Liturgy. He lost in this as well.

"They get along now, Kyle and Clara," I say, going back to the original conversation. Talking mates and relationships is opening old wounds. Falling in love is why I am here, how I lost everything. Jordan is right. Find out who you are first—a division—before you think about love.

"Yes." Jordan nods sharply, back to himself. "It has been some time since we have quarreled."

"Rebecca and I had a fight once," I admit, returning his candor with my own. Jordan raises his eyebrows, signaling for me to continue. I pull my feet out from under me and slide back to lean on the wall.

"When the Franklin's adopted me, I was barely thirteen. Vic was sixteen and Rebecca, nine. I couldn't believe my luck to find such a wonderful family. We spent so much time together, even with Vic away at boarding school and then college. He came home whenever he could, and the three of us were inseparable during summers. We spent so much time in the sun that Vic's hair turned nearly as blonde as Rebecca's." Pain tingles around the edge of my mouth as my face stretches into a wide smile. "For as long as I live, I will never forget those summers." The gravity of the promise clouds over my joy, killing my smile. I may live a hundred lives and won't forget them.

"You must have loved them very much. What could have gone wrong? You sound as if you were the perfect trio." I roll my eyes at Jordan's rare hint of sarcasm, but it works to push away the promise. I could get used to this Jordan. With a sigh, I continue.

"Rebecca never liked Janice, my best friend from the orphanage. At first it wasn't a problem because Janice wasn't around. At seventeen, she left the orphanage, and her first stop was to see me. I started sneaking out whenever I could to spend time with her. I felt like I owed Janice something for leaving her behind and getting a family. Even though we were both free of the orphanage, I had everything, and she only had me. Eventually I was careless with her visits.

"It was the summer after sophomore year, and I had been out late with Janice. There's a big tree outside of my bedroom, and that's how I would get in and out. As I was climbing back in, I slipped and broke my arm. When Judy and Peter asked, I said I slipped leaning out the window. Rebecca lied for me, and that was the last straw for her. She told me everything she'd been holding in about Janice. Repeating that Janice was no good and would bring me down. I yelled back too. I told her she couldn't keep me all to herself." I stop talking and take a couple breaths. Can I dream that memory and make it right?

"Who knows." I force myself to say what I've feared all along. "Maybe she did tell her parents about it. Not long after our fight, I was sent to boarding school."

Jordan leans toward me and cups a hand around the side of my face. It feels strong and soft against my skin. For the second time since becoming one of them, I let myself fall apart. Boarding school is what started it all. If I had just stayed home, we'd all still be together. The sadness I have been so carefully containing flows freely now.

"It sounds like Rebecca cared about you very much. All sisters fight. I hope you see her again, even if it is from a distance." Jordan kisses the top of my head gently.

My senses sharpen, and I bury the sadness. Clara and Kyle are heading back. Jordan notices as well and leaves a moment later.

Chapter 18

Clara

"Why are you always dragging me down here for your games?" Kyle asks as we approach the cell.

"It is not games," I reply coldly. "I am staying sharp, and you are learning vital skills." We take a few more steps, and I hear Kyle's lips move, shaping words without sound. "Just because I cannot see you, does not mean I do not know exactly what you are doing." I whip around to see Kyle mocking me. "Why do you impersonate me when we are alone?"

Kyle's face breaks into a smile. "I'm just enjoying the freedom to be myself while we are down here. When we rejoin society, I go back to being all business." Kyle drags open the cell door.

"You were funny even when you were a Guard." Though it is meant to console him, I make sure to sound as if simply stating it for the fact that it is. "And you were never all business." Kyle throws me a glare. I refocus on the high, flat edges of the cell walls and take a step back. With all my strength, I propel myself up the wall, fingers fighting to find a grip. My arms pull and repeat until I am up the wall.

"Before, I wasted away in the human world, guarding high-profile Dormants. Now I'm Guard to a Votary with the matched will of the Vegar," Kyle says from below.

"Have you truly thought about what Guard placement implies?" I ask and jump, letting myself drop to the bottom of the cell. "I am bored with this workout. I miss the court."

Kyle stares at me blankly. "You know I have," he says eventually, ignoring the second half of my statement.

"I do not think you have." Again, I squat and jump to the wall. This time I leap, traveling around the circumference of the cell. When I land beside Kyle, my arms ache a little. I am out of shape. "Still not getting it?" I ask with a bit of taunting in my voice.

For months I have been trying to tell him, and it can wait no longer. Kyle looks at me as if I am the one confused.

"If Angelica is a Slayer, then fine. Someday she may choose to vie for my place as Vegar. Or she is another strong soldier. What need does Krisenica have for a Guard with that much potential? The kind of Guard with a will to withstand anything or anyone?" Kyle's demeanor weakens, eyes focusing in concentration. "Can you think of any Guards that could stand against me?"

"You mean like the Téssera?" He exhales and loses an inch of his height as he droops. "No. The odds are too astronomical," he whispers. "Council members are of the purest Lymerian blood." Kyle is grasping for anything that allows Angelica to be a Guard and his forever.

"The fact something has never happened before does not mean it cannot happen. Look at her, Kyle," I say, softer this time because I know it will hurt him. "She even looks like the old Lymerians. The blood of the Elders made her into us."

Kyle is shaking his head in disbelief. "It was your idea to make the Council do that," he says accusingly.

"I know that. I wanted the best for my Votary, but we got more." Kyle stands to leave. He is done listening to me. "Kyle, it is in the scrolls," I say quietly.

"How long have you had them?" he asks without turning around, now completely deflated.

"They appeared in my room last year. As soon as I finished reading them, they were gone. Jordan does not know I have seen them. I wanted you to know first." The months gone by are evidence enough of their truth, because I could not bring myself to tell him, to hurt him.

"What do they say?" Kyle still refuses to look at me.

"*The time of Alternation draws near. It is hailed when the youngest among us matches the strongest between us*," I say, quoting the scrolls. Kyle finally turns with tears in his eyes. I already know what he is going to ask next. "*One will ascend from the beings below us.*" I finish.

"Why didn't you tell me?" Slumped and broken, Kyle's eyes beg me to help him understand.

"Because I knew how much it would hurt you."

"Since when has the Vegar ever cared about anyone's feelings?" Kyle shouts, anger quickly replacing his despair.

"Since she became an Architect," I answer. "There is no higher law. Nothing shall come between the three." Kyle's eyes soften—the anger in him short lived as always. "You love her so deeply. Just this once, I am a coward." Kyle crosses the cell in the blink of an eye and we embrace.

"Why haven't you told Jordan? The real reason." Kyle knows me well. There is more. I shake my head, feeling the emotion claw at my throat, threating to spill into my face. "No," he whispers and places his cheek on my head. "Did it say for sure?"

"*When three become two, their one becomes new.*" It was the final line. For months, I repeated the Liturgy scrolls that I committed to memory, praying for it not to mean us.

"No Lymerian ever born on Earth has died," Kyle assures me. The tears I have been battling break free. He means they have not died from natural causes, but we can be killed.

"An Alternation can only happen if there is . . ."

"Civil war," Kyle finishes. "Even if war comes, the scrolls don't give names. It could be any of us." I breathe properly for the first time in months. He is right. The scrolls did not name a person—Jordan felt like the one, though.

"What would cause such a war?"

The words I speak come from a part of my brain only the Astros can unlock, and I listen to myself with as much attention as Kyle. "There is unbalance between the Astros. When Liturgy began, the majority of Astros believed in preserving our kind. They no longer wished us to join the human race. Since then, you, me, and Jordan have all been born, along with hundreds of others. Astros were born among them as well, Kyle."

"Enough Astros have been born to cause an imbalance?" he asks.

"I do not know. I just know that their births have changed things." My mind is blocked when I try to think beyond what I have said. The information is there, but I cannot get to it. They have given me the answer, but it is not time for me to act on it.

"How do you know so much? It was not all in those scrolls."

"Thrice I have been called to Mountain Top, and I have very little memory of any visit. Each time I was gone for hours," I admit.

Kyle is quiet. He has heard the rumors of Astro abilities. "If you knew war was coming, who would be the one person you absolutely needed on your side?" Kyle offers.

"Anubis," I say.

"Or?"

"The Vegar." Seven years of dawdling in cells sheds itself from me. Suddenly I feel sharper and stronger, just as I was before Angelica heard my voice in the crowd.

"Imagine there are two sides to an argument spanning millennia. How could you end that argument?"

War. As a Slayer, I have been ready for war my whole life. I have fought in the human wars and kept aliens at bay, but never have we fought against ourselves.

"You believe Anubis and I will end up on different sides of the argument?"

"Have you ever agreed with Anubis?"

I see his point. Anubis and I have never gotten along. If the position of Vegar rested in his hands, I would not be the Vegar today. But everything has a reason for how it is done. Vegars are not chosen or appointed; they challenge for the honor.

"No one could control the outcome of the Vegar. I have been told that you nearly died winning your place." The memory of those final moments relives itself in my mind, every heartbeat on fast forward until my opponent is on his knees.

"Clara," Kyle says, forcing me back to the present.

"They want me to go against Anubis and the Council. I begin a civil war."

"You don't know that. We need to talk to Jordan."

When we return to our rooms, I tell Angelica to sleep. Then Kyle and I burst into Jordan's room. Jordan looks unhappy, but he will understand once we tell him our discovery.

"What now, you two?" Jordan is already taking the tone of annoyed older brother. Kyle can tell I am getting ready to fire back and begins talking before I can say anything.

"Not now, Jordan. Clara has seen the scrolls."

Jordan sits up, his attention immediately focused on what we are about to say. Kyle tells him what we have discovered without mentioning when I actually found the scrolls. When Jordan does not ask how long I have known, I am relieved. Jordan's place in our trio is not to question, but to mediate and guide.

Kyle finishes and Jordan is quiet for a long time. He is thinking, working it out inside himself. I want him to think out loud so I can hear every theory he has, even if they are awful. Years spent decision-making with Kyle has shown me time and time again that the best ideas are born of collaboration and team work. Jordan does not operate that way. Guards do not work in teams. They make individual decisions with only one objective in mind: *Keep my ward safe.*

"It changes nothing." Jordan looks from me to Kyle, and I know we are both staring back at him completely expressionless. "Liturgy is our law, and we must continue as we have been doing."

"We have to plan for every possible outcome of this." It is not a statement, but an urgent command.

"Clara, do you want to start a war? Do you wish to see your Slayers divided or dead for that matter?"

"No! Why would ask me that?"

"How can you start a war you do not want? You would never do anything to hurt your Slayers. You would lay down your life before you asked them to sacrifice theirs for you." Already my breaths are heavy at the thought of losing even one of my Slayers. He is right. "I agree that the only way there is civil war is if the Slayers are divided, and you and Anubis stand on opposite sides. Right now, I have no idea what chain of events could possibly lead to that outcome and neither do you. We must continue as we have. Anything out of the ordinary could ignite the spiral."

"The Astros showed her for a reason," Kyle offers.

"Exactly. This is their doing. We are but pawns in their game. There is great power in knowing information and refusing to act on it. This is Liturgy, and Angelica is all that matters. Whatever the Astros have planned, it is decades off. She is nowhere near ready to sit on the High Council."

"She's not even ready for the elevator." Kyle means it as a joke, an attempt to break the tension in the room. But neither Jordon nor I can be eased. "I'm going to get some sleep since she'll be out for a while." Jordan's silence gives Kyle his cue to leave. I turn to follow him.

"Stay." Jordan is not asking. He wants to keep me here to distract me from obsessing and configuring battle plans I will never use. But I cannot rest until I exhaust every path and every way around those paths. I look to the door, desperately wanting to move through it. Even more than wanting to leave, I want to stay. More than the need to plan is the need to be in his arms. In his arms, I am Clara and he is Jordan, just as it was so many lifetimes ago.

I stay, and we talk about Angelica and all the progress she has made until now. We become so engrossed in her that the threat of what is to come settles in the back of my mind. Jordan is right—whatever is coming is far off. Even so, her training is more important than ever. Finally, I understand why a Vegar is Architect.

War is coming, and everything we do must have reason, for it will be of great consequence.

Chapter 19

Angelica

It's been eight years since I've seen the moon and stars. I miss ice cream and pizza and lemonade. Stone walls and hard work are their crude substitutes. Things have accelerated with only one year until my next examinations. All day, every day, we work. Clara is aggressive and impatient with me. Physical training with her takes up all my time. Lessons are obsolete; there is nothing left to teach. A Lymerian memory and endless days devoured Kyle's and Jordan's knowledge.

I expected intensity and demanding from Clara and am not surprised by her change. The biggest difference is Kyle. His icy blue eyes once lingered on me whenever he was near. Now they stare, vacant, right through me. Gone is his playful tone and welcome laugh. I want the old Kyle back desperately. Our little moments of intimacy seem imagined, and I am emptier than in my cell. Jordan admitted Kyle's feelings for me, so what has changed? Despite Jordan's advice, I thought I could love him back. Maybe it could be forever.

The longer I'm here, the lonelier it gets.

They hardly give me any time to sleep. Lymerians can function with little sleep, and the time for sleep is over, they keep telling me. My dreams are becoming distant memories. Those precious years I had with Rebecca and Vic and the one amazing year I spent with Merrick are fading.

I wish I knew what happened to them. Rebecca is a woman now, older than I was when I disappeared. Did Janice ever settle down, have children to love? Did Vic marry his longtime sweetheart, Vanessa? Will I wake up one day and realize I haven't thought about them in decades? When will I stop caring?

"You will never stop caring." *Vic*. He is here, sitting on my dust-covered chair. "You care too much." My heart wants to leap with joy, but I smother it before it can miss a beat. "You are getting good at controlling that," Vic says, but he doesn't smile.

"What are you doing here?" I ask, grateful to see him even if this Vic isn't quite the one I remember. I can feel despair that never touched him in real life.

"It is easier to find you when you are thinking of me," he says flatly. Emotion is starting to fill me, and I have to force myself to breathe through it. This isn't Vic, just something from my head that reflects my own frustrations. "Why does that make you sad?"

"Because I know you aren't Vic. You're nothing like him. Where he was soft, you are stern. He smiled and you frown. You even sound different. I want the real Vic, my Vic. I need him."

"You did not know the real Vic. You knew the big brother that came home every weekend and played with his little sisters. Do you believe there was nothing more?" None of this makes sense. Have I gone so crazy that my mind has invented the anti-Vic to torture myself?

"You have not gone crazy—just finally seeing the truth with your superior Lymerian sight. You will start seeing everything more clearly now. Liturgy kills most humans. You are doing well but need to push harder."

"You sound like Clara." I smile to myself. It makes sense. Like a virus that infects the brain, the Lymerian cells are taking over my memories, using them to manipulate me. "You were nicer last time."

"That was . . . not like me." He pauses before meeting my eyes. "Do not give up on Kyle. He will never turn you away. He is scared of losing you because he is not enough for you."

"Then why should I be with him?" Explain that, Lymerian virus.

"He is your Guard. Keep him until you no longer need him." I shiver at the darkness in Vic, in me. How could I use Kyle that way? I won't. If I go to him, it will be because I want to love him.

I lie back down, trying to force myself awake. "You need to listen to Clara." Vic is next to me now, kneeling at the bed. "They are insistent with you because you are not progressing. Stop feeling sorry for yourself and finish your training. You have been down here too long."

I close my eyes again, and when I open them Vic is gone. For hours I lay in bed thinking about what he said. Part of me suspects Clara is playing a mind trick on me, using our connection. Maybe my Lymerian brain is more powerful than I thought. Can it trick me into working harder? Am I really behind? It makes sense. All three of them have gotten serious because we are running out of time. The only person holding me back is me.

My head jerks at the faint noise coming from down the hall—Kyle. With my decision made, I make myself move like them since I finally have a reason to. Before I can plan what to do next, I am sitting on his bed, staring down at him. Kyle is quicker than I've ever seen him as he lifts his arms to block whatever danger he senses. But I'm awake and snatch his wrists.

Now he knows it's me and relaxes as I lower his wrists. Vic is right; Kyle still wants to be with me. My lips find his, and he doesn't resist. His heart beat explodes beneath me. All the seemingly invisible ways a body reacts to this kind of closeness overwhelm my senses. For the first time in eight years, I find pleasure in what I've become. Then I think about Merrick and hesitate.

I will always cherish our first kiss and every kiss Merrick and I shared after it. I'll never forget Merrick, but I see one truth that I couldn't see before. Merrick said he loved me, but he never looked at me the way Kyle is looking at me.

Kyle pulls me back down hungrily, kissing me with twice the passion. Now my heart erupts into an erratic rhythm. For maybe ten seconds we lose ourselves until Kyle regains self-control.

"They can hear everything." That sobers me. I sit up and slide away from him. Kyle moves slowly out of bed. "I'm sorry" is all he has to say to me. What is he sorry for?

"Tell me more about you, like your real age." I'm afraid of losing him, of having him retreat from me again. There is so much he hasn't told me. Who Jordan, Clara, and Kyle are is still a mystery to me. I've learned that Jordan and Clara have known each other their entire lives. They were born in Greece together sometime during the first century. New Lymerians for a new era. Kyle is one of the youngest Lymerians and was born in a Nordic country. Maybe that is why he looks so pale compared to them.

"You know how old I am," Kyle says softly. "We don't count age by human years. Age isn't even a good word for it. Lymerians populate in surges, and I am part of the fourth. Clara and Jordan are from the first. We are soon approaching the fifth."

"Every five hundred years," I say and Kyle nods. "What's wrong?" Kyle's muscles are suddenly tense.

"Listen." I focus and let my mind differentiate between the four sets of noises. There are four beating hearts, shallow breaths along with four entirely different sets of bodily movements. Kyle is the loudest as he moves around the room getting ready. Jordan and Clara are both near, but not together. Jordan is motionless, but Clara is walking slow even steps. Every ten steps there is a pause before they start again.

"She is pacing?" I whisper to Kyle, then louder, "Are we keeping you waiting?" Now I'm annoyed. I don't want to leave this room and go back to all three of them taking turns torturing me—Clara with her training, Kyle and Jordan by their avoidance of me.

Kyle leaves without saying anything. What would he say? Goodbye? We are going to the same place and cannot escape being together.

By the time I finally walk out of Kyle's room, the others are gone. I sigh and charge down the pathway to my old cell. This will not be my fastest time, and Clara will be disappointed.

When I arrive at the open doorway, it is only Clara. "We need to talk about your examinations," she says quietly. "Remember the room where the Liturgy ceremony was performed." Images flip around in my head, locating the right one. Lymerian brains behave better than human ones. It always finds the answer if I look long enough.

"Yes."

"Your final examination will take place there. All Krisenica inhabitants will attend along with some Astros and nearly all Dormants. The Council will question you and there may be physical tests. I need to test your strength today." Clara's face is hard and unyielding. "Are you ready?"

For the next several minutes, I move without thinking, trying to stay out of her way as she executes attack after attack. Some of them I block, but the rest burn, bruise, and break different parts of my body. Anyone watching would have no idea that we have been training together daily for over three years.

"That's enough, Clara." Kyle is kneeling next to me, quickly checking me over.

"We are not done yet. All I know for sure, is she is no Slayer!" Clara shouts, anger ripping through the air and stabbing my heart. Sadness cripples me as I feel the depth of her disappointment. My body shakes, and I can't breathe.

"It is not your job to test her, Clara. You observe, train, teach, and make a recommendation to the Council for her placement." Jordan appears and stands between Clara and me. Then silence, except for the sobs that escape me every few seconds. The tension between the four of us pulses with our beating hearts. I know Clara will be angry with Jordan for what he just said, but I'm grateful. He's the only one who can reason with her. It's a long time before her boots start to click in the familiar pattern, but this time she's walking away from me. My sorrow starts to fade in harmony with her distance from me.

Jordan stares after her, wanting to follow, but he doesn't. Instead he turns back to me. His creese is out in a flash and against his skin. I welcome the warmth and sense of normal his blood gives me. Kyle's fingers tighten on my arm, but I don't care. My need for Jordan's blood is greater than the desire to spare Kyle's feelings.

"Do not leave her alone," Jordan instructs and follows Clara. Kyle helps me stand, and we move to the edge of the cell. Our rooms would be more comfortable, but Clara and I need distance right now. Kyle starts talking again, picking up his story where we left off earlier. He's trying to distract me, and it works.

"Being born, being young, isn't important to us. We don't even know which Lymerians we came from. When it's time for a surge, all females must have at least one offspring. Sometimes two are born from one female. Although we are near invincible on this planet when fully grown, our young are as fragile as humans. Many do not survive."

"What about the Dormants?"

"They return ten years before the surge begins. In the past, females became pregnant at different times spanning a decade or two. In the meantime, Dormants resume a diet of blood and regain their true form. When their offspring is born, they go back to the human world."

"Will they ever know if their child lived or died?"

Kyle shakes his head no. Orphans. They are all orphans.

"Do the others know? The Litmars, Guards, and Slayers?"

"No." Kyle pulls me closer to him.

"Why didn't you tell me before? Years of lessons, and I assumed we covered it all."

"I don't even know it all, Angelica."

I nuzzle closer to him, grateful for his massive size and ability to swallow my long limbs. "The next surge is going to be your first?" I ask quietly, finding another reason to want Kyle for my own. The thought of sharing him, even for this, infuriates me.

He shrugs. "There are less females than males and most have mates."

Will I be part of a surge one day? Every female is needed.

"You will never bear a child," he says, reading my thoughts. "You were not born Lymerian. Your body can bear neither Lymerian or human child. At least not that we have seen."

I think about Merrick and our plans for a family. The little girl that once pulled my emotions from the darkness wasn't mine at all. Another thing I must let go.

"Why don't you have more surges?" I ask, a new thought entering my mind. Why do they need Liturgy if they can reproduce? A familiar anger threatens to unbury itself. If they can have children, there is no reason for human replacements. There was no need for me.

"Females are only fertile once every five hundred years. We've tried, Angelica. Fertilization happens on the same cycle. Nature's way of keeping our population down, I guess. It wasn't like this when Lymerians arrived on Earth. Once we stopped feeding on humans and became long-lived, our bodies stopped reproducing. The Astros predicted with eerie accuracy when reproduction would return. They called it the surge."

And not all survive—I bolt upright. No wonder we skipped over Lymerian reproduction. "Clara had a mate once, right?"

Kyle nods. "None of their children survived. They lost three." The anguish I should have felt at my own sterile fate hits me full on. She lost *all* of her children. "It tore them apart." I move swiftly. One moment I'm on the floor next to Kyle, and the next, I'm back at our rooms.

"Your fastest time yet," Clara's resigned voice sounds from the darkness of her room. Jordan is not with her. I wait in the doorway; it doesn't feel right to enter without being invited. "Do not feel sad for me." She knows Kyle told me, doesn't want my sympathy or understanding.

"I'm sorry I'm not doing better," I say. I should be sorry for that.

"Do not be sorry. You are who you are."

My earlier injuries are catching up with me, so I turn to find my own bed. I'm not needed here, and my body needs to rest. Just before I leave, Clara gives me a final lesson, one that I know will make sleep difficult.

"Be careful with Kyle. You have opened a door with him, and you will find it does not easily shut."

Chapter 20

Clara

Our time here is nearing its end. After more than nine years, Angelica looks like one of us, moves like one of us, and thinks like one of us. Yet she still does not believe she is one of us. We are out of lessons and done with drills. What she needs cannot be taught here. It is time for her to be assigned a division, surrounded by those most like her for progress to continue. She needs more distance between her human life and Lymerian one. Time and our kind will help her.

"Where are you going?" Jordan asks from the edge of his room. He sees me staring at the barred elevator.

"To see Farrell," I reply and remove the first board. Jordan joins me and together we pull apart the barricade. Kyle and Angelica are listening to us, but stay still. They are together in Kyle's room.

"Are you sure? Once she goes upstairs, she is out of your hands." He means everything will be out of our hands. Jordan believes I will abandon him once I am with the Slayers again, and I am equally sure he will return to his mate. But it is the law. The tenth year approaches.

"Protocol is for the four us to continue to live in close proximity. Together, we will introduce Angelica to our way of life, and in time she will find her place among her division. We have less control, but nothing will change between us." I am both soft and stern as I say this to him.

Jordan has to stoop for his tall frame to meet my small one, so that he can gently place his lips on mine. As he starts to pull away, I lean in and with more force, bring my lips back to his. I use this moment to unlock my buried emotions for him, to show him what he means to me. A Vegar cannot show emotion like this once we go upstairs. He replies ravenously, gripping my hair tightly and digging his fingers into my side, his true passion grateful to be set free.

*   *   *

It is different this time as I walk through the archways of Krisenica. Word spreads fast that I am on the surface, and everyone knows it can only mean one thing—the Votary is ready. Angelica's ability during the Ceremony did not go unnoticed, and she is my Votary. Will they believe that she is different, stronger than the other Votaries, or will they rely on history to predict their future?

Instead of going to the Litmar wing, I set out for the court. Coming home feels right. Though I am worried about Angelica joining the real Krisenica, I selfishly yearn to come back to this place for good. It will be a challenge splitting my time between her and the Slayers when there is not a barred elevator between us. If she is Slayer, I need not worry. The scrolls threaten to distract me, whispering their prophecy and begging for action. It is easy to wipe them away now that I am home, and I am Vegar.

The court is close and too quiet—devoid of Slayers. I listen to the other sounds Krisenica offers, searching for them. The gymnasiums have the appropriate amount of Guards, with more stationed throughout Krisenica on patrol. Not that Slayers would ever be in a gymnasium. Litmars buzz quietly on their side of the mountain. There are no other groups gathered within Krisenica. The Slayers are not here, which means . . . My face flashes with anger, and I am very lucky no one is near to see it. I close my eyes again and listen hard. There are three still in the court. I move.

"Why are you not with your Slayers?"

Samuel startles but hides it well from the other two. Leif and Nina immediately leave the room. Samuel does not answer because the answer is obvious—he is no longer in charge of the Slayers. He was left behind in case I surfaced, so that the situation could be explained to me by a captain.

"They are with the Tolken," he admits.

"Clearly," I say evenly. I could call the Tolken, the second strongest Slayer, and he would have no choice but to return from wherever they are immediately. That would only make things worse.

"I am surprised at his early return," I say, my tone heavy with contempt. Samuel does not reply. He knows better than to speak against the Tolken. Only Anubis and I have that privilege. Out of habit, I pace, thinking about the Tolken and why he has returned.

"Your Votary is ready for the examinations then?" Samuel asks, changing the subject. I glare at him. "And how is Jordan?" Samuel's trained eyes discern my choice—the evidence is all over me.

"Tell the Tolken he shall have no part in this. That is an order from his Vegar."

Samuel stands straight, my tone telling him all he needs to know. Whatever was once between us is gone, and I doubt Samuel will ever speak in such a familiar way to me again. He is a true soldier.

"It shall be done."

Slowly I make my way to the opposite side of Krisenica, to the Keeper. To be gifted with such speed and not use it is incredibly irritating. I want to tear through the halls and steal into his office, just to remind him that I can. The return of the Tolken has lit a fire in me. His presence could ruin everything we have done these past nine years.

"You have good news for me, Vegar?" Farrell's distinct timbre reaches me long before I walk through the archway to his office. He is in a good mood, a rarity for him. I imagine it has much to do with my sour one. Farrell feeds off the disappointment of others.

"You may call back the Dormants and make a formal request to the High Council. We have done all we can below the surface. It is time."

"Right on schedule; the tenth year approaches."

"Indeed." I turn to leave.

"Are you nervous? Is she everything we hope her to be? All of Krisenica is buzzing to catch a glimpse of the Votary that attacked Anubis. He will not go easy on her."

"Nor should he," I reply confidently. "Her will is equal to mine. I am not sure he could go easy if he tried."

"And what of you, Vegar? Ready to return to your Slayers? I am sure you have heard the Tolken is back sooner than expected. Have you told her yet? I doubt you have. Pity." Farrell actually smiles as he says it. Pathetic. Still, I am Vegar and must behave as so.

"Farrell, you know very well that I am not at liberty to discuss Slayer matters with those outside of our division."

"You know that it is not what I meant." He pauses and leans back in his chair. I turn to leave. "Do you mean to say she is not a Slayer?" Farrell's tone sounds genuinely intrigued by that prospect.

"No one is a Slayer until the Council rules it so. Do you have all you need to begin the process?" Farrell stares at me and after several seconds, nods. I take my leave before he can say anything else.

There is one last stop before my return to the dungeons. It is unplanned, but with the return of the Tolken, necessary. Completely alone in the stairwell, I am free to climb at my speed. What awaits me has no visitors. They hear me coming, and the Téssera move to the entrance. When I reach the top of the stairs, I knock three times.

"Who calls?" The deep voice thunders through the walls, one of the Téssera. *Formalities.*

"Vegar Clara." As if they do not know who calls.

A pause and voices so hushed, even I can barely hear.

"Why have you come here, Clara?" Anubis's voice is close. The door is sealed, yet he is on my side. There must be another exit, or Etherial helped him. I turn and face him.

"Why was the Tolken allowed back?" I demand.

"He thinks he can be of assistance to you and your Votary."

"That is not his decision to make, nor yours." Anubis understands the Laws of Liturgy as well as anyone.

"You could not be reached to confer." A true but slippery statement.

"I do not want him anywhere near her. That is my order." Anubis sucks in air—a mistake. Slayers cannot show emotion, especially when speaking to a subordinate. I have made him angry. Good.

"You presume to order me, child." Anubis's voice is raised. Something stirs on the other side of the wall—his Guard.

"I may order anyone that attempts to interfere with Liturgy." Both of our hearts stop beating as we fight to remain in control of our emotions. "He stays out of it."

"The Tolken is powerful. If your Votary has strength to equal yours, we may have no choice but to use him."

The blood in my veins turns to ice as I retreat. Anubis's logic is sound. The Tolken has been allowed back because they fear what I have created these past years in the dungeons. I think of the scrolls. Who else has read them?

* * *

All three are waiting for me in Jordan's room when I return from the surface. I join them and sit next to Jordan on his bed. Our days here are finally numbered. In the beginning, it felt as if I had been given a prison sentence. Years in isolation with two Guards and a human—no Slayer would want that. This Slayer wanted it less than any being in Krisenica, but Angelica was given to me anyway.

Liturgy changed everything. Now I could not bear to lose her or Jordan. Even Kyle has found a way into my blackened heart. Will Jordan keep his promise? As time goes on, his desire to be near me and protect me will lessen. My coldness and dedication to my Slayers will drive him back into Karina's waiting arms. I cannot keep him. He was never my mate. My mate is gone.

"What happens next?" Angelica whispers. Kyle's empty eyes meet mine.

"Lymerians will be summoned to Krisenica. It will take time to gather them. Eventually, we will be summoned too. The Council will meet you alone and ask a series of questions. Afterward they will confer, and I will be called in to offer my recommendation. The physical test will be next."

"Will I have to fight?"

Kyle tenses and Angelica looks at him, her eyes wary.

"It depends," Jordan offers.

"Potential Slayers and Guards must fight. Dormants do not. I have never seen a Litmar come out of Liturgy," Kyle says, knowing it is better if she hears the truth. She is going to have to fight. Angelica takes a deep breath in acknowledgement of his words.

"You have nothing to be afraid of, Angelica," I say fiercely. "Nothing can stop you when you put your entire mind, body, and soul into it."

"Could you stop me? Not because you are my Architect. If you weren't and didn't have control over me, could you stop me?"

For several seconds I stare at her, and then my face widens into a rare smile. The night I read the scrolls, I remembered my youth. "No Slayer can best me—but you might not be a Slayer." We all look at each other, agreeing that Angelica is Slayer or Guard. We cannot properly test her down here. She refuses to unleash herself on me, and Jordan and Kyle cannot fight unless defending.

"In practice, a Guard cannot defeat a Slayer one to one or even two to one. But that is practice. A real test would require a Slayer to attack a Guard's ward. Even then, Slayer would likely win."

"Unless the Guard loved their ward." Jordan's triumphant eyes meet mine.

"I could not beat you though," Kyle says, missing the exchange.

"You and I are not of equal will and strength," I reply. Also, Angelica was not in true danger.

"But you and Angelica are or will be one day," Jordan states, moving us closer to the answer.

"What does that mean?" Angelica's voice is soft and desperate, as if one day she would actually have to stand against me. Perhaps if she believes she can best me, then she will not fear anyone.

"It means that once you are fully trained, you could beat me if I was attacking someone you loved. Although equally matched, your will to save them would be stronger than my desire to kill them."

That night, we sleep at the same time. No more sleeping and training in shifts. We will spend all of our waking hours together. Every moment is precious.

While we wait for the summons, we continue our training routines. Angelica practices combat with all three of us, even Kyle. The thought of fighting for her place among Lymerians changes something in her. We hold back, focusing on her technique and form instead of her strength. Her strength will come when she has need of it.

Jordan reviews the important inhabitants in Krisenica, what they do and how old they are. He dissects the divisions down to the lowest rankings. He knows little about Dormants, so Kyle fills in the gaps. Kyle finds new stories and histories to tell Angelica to keep her distracted as each day we get closer to her exams.

We go on like this for six months.

Chapter 21

Angelica

"What is your name?" Valencia goes first. She is the Dormant and perfectly sculpted into the ideal modern woman. Her shiny blonde hair is big, shaping her face in a wave and held tight with hairspray. Makeup layers her soft face. Black liner and blue eyeshadow corral her big brown eyes. For my exam, she wears the Dormant green cloak. Underneath, a dress of the latest fashion, perhaps. The other council member's cloaks reflect their divisions too. My cloak is red, but soon it will be replaced with my division color.

Valencia is the council member that doesn't make sense. How is she allowed on the Council while living in the human world? Her post is top secret, known only by the Council, Isaac, the Keeper, and her Guard. I look at the four Guards that sit behind the others. Is one Guard all she needs? The crisp, smooth-shaven, dark haired man closest to her must fit in among humans as well. Many Guards must pass for human. I want to keep thinking about how it all works, but I'm here to answer their questions, not have my own.

"Angelica," I say, bringing my focus back to the moment. No last names. Lymerians have no last names. They have titles and positions. I suppose it makes sense as last names are family names. The Lymerians do not have blood family.

"Do you want to return to the human world?" That's not what I expected—choice. In my cell, I would have said yes. Going home to the Franklins was all I wanted. But after ten years, I am not the same. I can't go back.

"What would I do?"

"Placement is determined by many things. You are of little use to us as you are; we would need to educate you, give you a skill that benefits our race. What did you like doing before?"

"I liked spending time with my family."

Valencia smiles. "Good. Perhaps you could marry someone of importance in the human world. Tall, lean, and exotic—very desirable to simple men. A widower with children perhaps, as you shall bear none of your own." Valencia smiles again and looks down the line of Council members triumphantly.

No. No more new families. Clara, Kyle and Jordan are my family now, and I'm not going to leave them. "I don't want a human family, and I never liked humans." The words come easily, because they are true.

Valencia doesn't press me any further; she believes me. After a slight nod, she turns her head to signal that she is done questioning me. I've discovered a Lymerian truth: Dormants must want to live in the human world.

"Do you think it is fair, what has happened to you?" Reina, the Litmar, asks questions next. While her skin is ashy gray, eyes yellow and slanted like Anubis's, her hair is long and brown with sparkling gray streaks—humanlike. She must be very old, possibly the oldest one on the council. It makes sense that a law maker would be an elder, even among such a long-lived race.

Valencia and Reina are the only women. The Guards, Etherial, and Anubis are all men. Etherial is missing. Beyond noticing the black of his Slayer cloak, I pay Anubis no notice.

"I've spent years thinking about that, reliving every moment that led me to this place. There is no one to blame but myself. I had a choice, every time." She is still staring at me; I haven't answered her question. "More than fair when death was the alternative." Again, I speak the truth. Human and Lymerian still wage war inside me, but Lymerian won the battle to live despite my final words to Merrick.

"Has the Vegar been fair to you during your training?" I see a theme here.

"Training is not supposed to fair. She has been thorough, crafty, intelligent, and superior during every moment of my training." Reina smiles at this answer. She likes Clara.

"If you could change one of our laws, which one would you change and why?"

"I don't know all your laws; ask me again when I've learned them." Snicker from the right, a Guard. It makes me think of Jordan.

"All right, pick a human law then."

Now I snicker. "Just one?"

Valencia laughs softly. Reina doesn't get the joke.

"Enough," Anubis interjects. "Liturgy does not produce Litmars."

"Stating something has never happened is not a reason to support its impossibility," Reina replies calmly.

"No. Just a high improbability," Anubis counters firmly.

"Or the inverse. A Litmar from Liturgy is long overdue." Reina takes the final word, a new power residing in her voice that makes Anubis stay silent.

Reina continues her questions, and I do my best to answer honesty. Lying isn't an option. If they catch me changing my position, it will make Clara look bad. Jordon often reminds me how important and respected Clara is. He never said everything I do will be judged by the highest standard, but it's what he implied.

So far, I have not seen Clara interact with anyone above the surface. The hallways were clear as we made our way to the stairwell that leads to the Council quarters—no one can see me until the arena. At the top of the stairs, the door was open and I walked in alone. I desperately want to see how everyone else sees her.

Eventually Reina is satisfied. It doesn't seem like I've misstepped as I purposely did with Valencia. Reina collected everything she could from me. She seems determined to prove to Anubis that a Litmar can come from Liturgy. Maybe I should have lied.

Anubis is next, but instead of beginning, he waves a hand.

"You are not asking any questions?" Reina's tone is sharp, making it clear she doesn't like this.

"I do not need to. She is no Slayer." Anubis looks right at me when he says this, daring me to jump to his side of the room and prove him wrong. A piece of me wants to. "I can see it in her eyes."

These docile pale eyes hide the rage burning beneath them at his dismissal of me. I'm working hard to control all of my other body parts as well. I hate him. It was smart to ignore him before. Otherwise my focus for Valencia and Reina would have been shattered. Ten years has done nothing to soften the memories of the night he dragged me out in front of all of Krisenica and killed Merrick.

A dull thud draws everyone's attention to the left side of room. Another thud follows. "Ah, Etherial shall join us now." I take advantage of the distraction to ground myself, remembering that all of them can detect any physical reaction I have.

Etherial leans on a walking stick and is dressed in gold robes, the color of the Astros. He is neither human nor Lymerian in features—he is more like me. His skin is pale, like an albino, and hair white. This creature is very old. The thin hair, rough skin, and slow step tell the story of something that has lived far beyond what it should. All at once it hits me. Etherial was not born on this planet. He is an alien of another world. On his planet, he would have lived a short life, but on this one he can't seem to die.

"Welcome, Angelica," Etherial says in a high, soft voice as he takes his seat next to Anubis. His kind words relax the tension inside me. Our eyes meet, and I'm startled to see his large eyes are as white as his hair. This one feature makes him look undeniably other worldly.

No one has welcomed me here, not even Clara. With two words, Etherial makes me feel like he genuinely wants me to be here. From somewhere far away in the depths of my mind, I hear Rebecca's childish laugh. She welcomed me with open arms when I joined her family. Rebecca wanted me there, and it made all the difference.

"This is precisely why we have strict rules about Astros interacting with Votaries. You should not have come; we can settle this ourselves." Anubis sours my one moment of acceptance. I hate him even more, if that's possible. The voice in my head that used to be my constant companion in the cell whispers, *He knows how you feel about him too.* Anubis can't be trusted. It doesn't matter if he's on the Council. He is against me.

Forcing myself to focus, I look back to Etherial's white eyes and say, "Thank you."

"If Etherial is here, he has his reasons. Let us move on," Reina says, but Anubis is nowhere near done sabotaging me.

"Angelica, you may return to the others for a few minutes. They will bring you to the arena when it is time." Anubis speaks with slightly less hostility in voice this time. Etherial has a positive effect on him whether he likes it or not. Maybe it isn't what he said to me that made me happy. Maybe it's just him being near. The Council members start to shift in their chairs.

It's over. How can it be over? It doesn't make sense. Why is Etherial here if he isn't asking questions? I glance to the Guards. They haven't asked questions either. What if I'm a Guard?

Anubis, looking incredibly annoyed as he catches the questions clouding my eyes, says, "Etherial does not need to ask questions. He saw you and that is enough. The Guards will get a vote, but they have no questions for you as your Architect is a Slayer."

I bite my tongue so hard I taste blood. *But what if I'm a Guard,* I want to scream. They didn't ask any questions! We had not planned for me to end up with the Litmars. I'd rather be a Dormant than here without Clara or Kyle. *Calm.* I hear the word in my head, but it isn't my inner voice. It's Clara. She is not far and needs me to calm down.

The doors behind me open, and Clara, Jordan, and Kyle walk in. Clara takes her place next to me, Jordan to her right, and Kyle to my left. When we all stand together, it feels like nothing can harm us. My panic disappears, washed away with the strength of the others. Does the Council feel it too? Etherial is smiling, Anubis frowns, Valencia looks terrified, and Reina is expressionless.

"Clara. It is so good to see you again." Clara nods briefly at Etherial but doesn't fall under his spell like I did. Her eyes are cold, all business. This is the Vegar I've been hearing about. I glance at the Council, wanting to know how they see her. Watching their faces won't give me any answers. Valencia is the only one who wears her emotions. Jordan's tracking lesson comes back to me. Tracking can be used to sense emotion and uncover lies.

In theory, I should be able to handle this. My tracking skills have improved over time. Reach out with my energy and absorb theirs. Tracking can be used over long distances; what I'm doing is much easier than that. The Council is right in front of me and distracted by Clara. Quickly, I reach, wanting to finish before anyone else can speak. Valencia and Reina feel nervous, maybe even scared. Their Guards are buzzing, containing massive amounts of energy. Each of them are alert, ready for the threat—Clara. Anubis is emotionless or blocking me.

The moment I reach for Etherial, I hear his sweet voice in my head. *There you are.*

I pull back and sense a Guard tracking me. They are all staring at Clara, leaving me to guess who.

"Vegar, do you have a recommendation for us?" Reina asks. Clara nods and lifts her hand with a slip of paper in it. One of the Guards steps forward, takes it, and walks it to Reina. Reina accepts the slip and says, "Thank you. Please go to the arena."

No one says anything as we walk down the many flight of stairs. When we reach the bottom, Jordan stops at the door.

"The door is soundproof," he announces.

Clara turns and starts to give instruction. "You will be on your own, Angelica. Kyle will be close but restrained. He will be very dangerous when the fighting begins. Slayers and Guards will line the outer rim of the arena, alternating. They are there to keep you in and others safe. The Dormants are fragile, and the Litmars are easy targets."

"Why?" is all I can get out. What do they think is going to happen? This is supposed to be an exam.

"They must prepare as if they are unleashing me upon the crowd. You are my Votary; security is relevant to my strength."

Clara knew all along it would be like this. "You should have told me."

"No, I should not have," Clara replies icily. Is this who she will be now? I turn to Kyle, hoping that I haven't lost him too. His face is red and sweating. "Jordan, take Kyle."

"Wait, I want to say goodbye." I try to push past Clara. Jordan already has Kyle in his grasp.

"Why?" Clara moves an inch, more than enough to let me know I need to stop. "The exam will be over quickly. We will be together soon." Clara is confident and cruel in her promise. Kyle looks at me one last time before Jordan pulls him out the door.

"Where will you be?" I manage to say, my focus barely still here. I want to leave, to run. Ten years hasn't changed anything. Stepping into the arena feels exactly the same. Clara knows I'm starting to lose it but doesn't seem to care.

"The Architect is supposed to be restrained but none dare try. I will watch from above. I cannot help you as I did the night of the ceremony. You will be entirely on your own until the Council decides it is over. Angelica, look at me." Clara reaches up with her small hand. Her fingers dig into my neck as she pulls my face close to hers. "You are one hundred times more capable than you were that night. The moment you believe in your strength, there will be none that can stop you." She lets me go and steps to the door.

"Clara," I choke.

"You are being weak, Angelica. You are not weak." She gathers my long hair and tucks it in my hood. "Remember that all wounds heal. Take that door. It leads to the arena." She points behind me, and I see a door that I didn't before. I look back the way we came, to the Council's private chambers. Is this their entrance to the arena? When I turn back, Clara is gone. I step through the door and wish for the thousandth time that I'd never met Merrick.

This route to the arena is short, reminding me that this time will be different. Today I'm strong, fast, and willing. It's quiet, and for a second I pretend I won't have to do this in front of all of them. I listen harder until I hear their shallow breathing and tapping hearts—hundreds of them. They are so quiet, standing like statues, barely breathing in and out. I'm through thc archway, making my way to the center of the floor as Clara told me. All they see is a figure in a red cloak and hood. Votaries wear red, the color of life for the Lymerians.

I raise my eyes to catch a glimpse of the crowd. They are all cloaked and hooded—invisible, silent observers. When I reach the center of the room, I stop and track for Kyle and Clara. Kyle is close and distressed. I push farther and farther out, searching for Clara. Eventually I catch a piece of her but lose it when I hear the Council coming. Their path takes them to a set of chairs high above the arena.

"Remove your hood." I don't recognize this Council member. His deep voice whispers the words slowly, like it takes a lot of effort. It's a Guard speaking from the shadows. They are behind the others again. I remove my hood and let my white hair fall down. Faint whispers tickle my ears. I expected this. They see nothing of the girl that begged for her life ten years ago.

Use that to your advantage, Clara had coached me.

Silver hair and translucent skin were all I could see. Without a mirror to reflect the other changes, Kyle described my barely blue eyes and nearly white lips. My hair is now long and shimmery from years of unimpeded growth. As long as I feed, my veins stay hidden beneath pale skin. I yearn to see with my own eyes. Could I even pass for human now?

"The Council offers the placement of Litmar." The room erupts with many different sounds, and I almost forget to panic. *Not the Litmars*. Silence falls as the assembled and I wait for more. "As with all Litmar placements, each Litmar shall be given a vote to accept or deny this placement." Blue cloaks rise up between greens, grays, and blacks. One by one they murmur assent. My heart drops as the blue cloaks slide back into their seats.

Reina bows slightly before the Guard continues. "The Architect has offered a different recommendation. The Laws of Liturgy are clear. If the Architect and Council do not favor similar placements, the Votary shall be tested for both accordingly. The Votary has already passed the Litmar test, having received majority approval vote from the Litmars. Therefore, the Votary will now be tested as a Guard."

Now it makes sense. A Guard is leading the exams because I am being tested for placement into his division. *Breathe,* I tell myself.

Three soft plinks announce the three Slayers that are here to make sure Clara is right in her recommendation of my division. Do they know that if they succeed, that means their Vegar is wrong? *Never has an Architect been a Vegar,* Clara said once. All three sling their black cloaks to the side. I do the same.

Information about my opponents pours into my head. One female and two males. The female is Kyle's surge with the same light skin and hair. The dark-skinned man looks like a warrior with muscles bulging from his sleeveless tunic. His purple eyes make me wonder what blood runs through his veins. The final Slayer is tan with dark hair and yellow eyes, older than even Clara.

"Three of you?" I taunt before I can stop myself. Purple Eyes smiles at me.

"We'll start with one and see how you do. Slayers prepare for everything," the female says. They start to circle, and I get the feeling that they will not be easy on me. The two males fall back slightly and the screaming starts. *Kyle.* I dart to the side of the arena, toward the screams, taking advantage of the gap between the Slayers. I don't see him. He must be behind a door. One of the Slayers catches up to me and strong hands throw me across the room. I land easily and move again, avoiding them, needing to get to Kyle. The longer I take, the more pain they'll put him through. His next set of screams are louder.

The female catches up to me and pain instantly burns across my side. Running to Kyle won't work—they are faster. First, I have to fight them before I can help Kyle. How will I fight them all? They don't give me time to make a plan. A hundred lessons sweep through my mind as I defend their attacks.

Defend is all I manage, just like in the dungeons when fighting Clara. After several minutes, I'm still fighting three of them. Kyle's screams are closer together, and I'm losing focus. Maybe I am a Litmar. Shouldn't I be in Guard mode? Aren't I supposed to be as capable as Clara? It's taking everything I have to keep up with them. Clara and I never practiced fighting multiple opponents. Jordan and

Kyle wouldn't fight against me until the very end. A lot of good that did me.

"You do not deserve to be her Votary," Purple Eyes says before swinging me far across the arena. I'm ready for it and land smoothly. Then, new screams fill the arena, and they are not Kyle's. They sound like a child's screams . . . like *hers*.

"Angelica! I'm here!" It's Rebecca, unmistakably. When I hear her voice, something inside my core changes. For the first time, I am *awake*. Why would they have Rebecca? Do they want to take her, another replacement? *Never.*

The three Slayers surround me. I dive at the oldest one and in a single motion, grab and swing him by his feet. His body hits the two others hard. I spin us around again and let the Slayer fly into the crowd. There's not time for me to be surprised at my strength and speed. I have to finish the others. They come at me together.

All of Clara's teachings are like second nature to me. We drilled for years so when the time came I could just do. Their attacks are no match for me. As soon as the female steps too close, I break her arm and then her neck. The arena stills. Purple Eyes steps back from me. Is he giving up?

Then my skin goes cold, and the hair on my arms stand up. Something very dangerous is near me. I turn around and put all my strength into one attack. My arms hit a brick wall. But it's not a brick wall, its two hands, strong hands blocking my hit. I can't see my opponent because they are cloaked in black.

"Angelica! Please!" Rebecca screams again. My legs have the most power, so I try to use them. No matter how I move, he's faster, blocking me. *Let your opponent underestimate you.* Clara's instructions, along with a dozen other thoughts on how I can best this Slayer circle in my mind. I let up, just a little, and he thinks he has me. He goes to strike. I lift my leg and deliver a huge kick to his exposed stomach, where they are most vulnerable.

His attack breaks my arm, but my hit brings him down. Now I have two choices: run to Rebecca or try to finish this Slayer. *She's in the Council's tower.* I have to run, I have to find her. There are Slayers blocking my way, but I don't slow down.

"No. She is mine," a voice shouts from behind me, and the others fall back. I recognize the voice instantly, and my need to fight vanishes. My feet stop moving, and the Slayer collides into me with all his strength.

"No!" I scream as I skid across the floor, an eruption of pain moving through my shoulder and knees. He stops quickly, understanding too late that it's over. This game is over. The throbbing throughout my body begs for my attention. He's walking away, getting away. *All wounds heal.* I use Clara's words to force myself to my unsteady knees, because he's not leaving me.

"Stop," I order and the figure, still hooded, stops. "Show me your face, coward!" Anger is fueling me now. Rebecca is not in danger, and he will turn around. "I deserve to see your face," I growl at him. *Heal,* I beg my body and start to stand. Years of forcing myself to heal without blood has trained my Lymerian body well. Slowly I limp to the hooded figure. He turns and removes his hood.

My heart collapses as I look into his eyes. They are so like Clara's, cold and emotionless. Why didn't I see it before?

"I am not a coward," he says. Tears leak down my face, but I don't care. It was all lies. Everything that has happened to me since I left the orphanage was a lie. This was their plan for me. I just couldn't see it until now. In a breath, the sadness spilling from me turns to rage.

"Where's Merrick?" I say through gritted teeth. He turns from me and begins to walk away. "Victor!" I shout. "Don't you dare walk away from me!" All of Krisenica is still watching quietly, even the Council, but I don't care. My body is healing enough for me to charge. He turns and grabs my arms, but it's not a fair fight. He's barley trying to hold me back. With nothing to fight for but my own pride, I am nothing against him. "Where's Merrick?" I scream again and catch a flicker of the old Vic in his eyes.

"That's enough," Clara commands, and both of us obey immediately. Vic turns to leave again. "Tolken. Stay," Clara says smoothly. Only I, as her Votary, sense her rage burying itself beneath her outward calm. We are almost one despite her betrayal. Vic turns around without looking at her or me. He is a Slayer, and she is his Vegar.

The Vegar looks straight at me, but there are no apologies in her eyes. There is everything in mine. She turns to face the Council. I do the same even though I should be screaming at them to tell the truth. Everyone lied, is lying to me, even Clara, Jordan, and Kyle. They knew everything all along.

Still, I don't scream. That's what a human would do. The war is won. I'm Lymerian. I know it because I can stand here and swallow my heartache and devastation, because Clara told me to stop. Whether it's our link or my Lymerian brain that keeps me in line, I don't know.

"The Council accepts her placement as Guard," the overseer says. And just like that, it is over. The Council files out first and within seconds the arena is empty except for Clara, Vic, and me. As Jordan and a bloody Kyle walk to us, Victor stiffens. I don't feel sorry for Kyle; it's nothing compared to what I've been through. To his credit, he doesn't try to comfort me.

Clara holds a hand up before I can interrogate them. "We will explain, but not here."

"The giza is closest," Vic says and starts to walk toward one of the exits. I'm so angry that following his lead seems like siding with the enemy. My own anger is cut short when I sense Clara's disgust. I look from her to Vic and realize something is very wrong between the two of them. What does it mean that she called him Tolken?

Chapter 22

Angelica

A few minutes later all five of us are crowded in a strange room, the walls black with tar and feel prickly to the touch. Aside from that, it is normal, set with a table and several chairs. No one sits.

"For privacy—nothing can get in," Vic says, and I throw him a glare for knowing what I'm thinking.

"Where's Merrick?" I ask again now that we are safely behind these walls or whatever they are.

"Why is that your first question? What of Rebecca's safety?" Vic has some nerve talking to me after pretending for years, helping to steal my life away. This Slayer in front me isn't the Vic I knew. He doesn't even sound like that Vic, but being a Lymerian now, I'd know him in any disguise.

"Angelica, it is better if you stay calm." I whip my head around, ready to accuse Clara of lying to me all these years, but the moment our eyes meet, I deflate. She's dropped the Vegar act and looks like my Architect again. I glance from Vic to Clara. She isn't afraid to be herself around him.

"Rebecca is fine," I say, turning back to the wall. Both of them make me sick.

"How could you know?" Vic isn't letting it go. Fine. I'll bite.

"Because I'm a Guard, and we know when the people we care about are safe and when they are in danger. A *Slayer* wouldn't understand." I sneer at the word *Slayer* like it's some disease I might catch. But I've spent years learning about the Lymerians, and Guards and Slayers do not get along. Already I am sure Vic despises Guards. His demeanor in the arena changed when Jordan and Kyle approached. I can't hurt Vic the way he's hurt me, but I can piss him off.

I'm right about Rebecca, because I truly am a Guard. Deep down I've known for a while, but having the Council confirm my division elevates my confidence. Even Jordan has been easy to track this past year.

Vic stares at me for several seconds before he says, "She took a great risk helping you tonight." I think about that. "A threat to the Guard's life was not quite enough motivation for you." Vic looks over to Kyle, taunting him, eyes brimming with hatred. A piece of me shatters to see his kind eyes used as such a weapon.

"Will she be punished?" I ask. Kyle scoffs and Vic tenses.

"Astros do not receive punishments," Jordan says neutrally before either Kyle or Vic can respond. "Their kind are too rare to harm."

Rebecca's an Astro—that makes sense. Her kind heart, sensitivity to others, keen intuition. That means Judy and Peter are also Lymerians and living in Krisenica. Suddenly it hits me. Peter is Rebecca's Guard—she always belonged to him. Judy was extra protection, even Vic probably. There are so many layers to my past, my head is spinning.

"She really has you wrapped around her finger, doesn't she, Tolken?" The light heartedness in Kyle that I've grown so found of over the years is gone. "This is exactly why Astros are not allowed prolonged interaction with us." Kyle is accusing someone of something, but I'm not sure who or what.

"I asked a question!" I shout. "I don't want to talk about Rebecca right now, I want to talk about Merrick." All four of them go quiet. Clara folds her arms and starts to pace. Vic sits down and puts his foot up on another chair—a habit from his human days. Kyle looks down. Only Jordan meets my eyes.

"None of them want to talk about Merrick," Jordan says quietly.

"Is he alive?" I say, feeling the tears starting to come back. Jordan nods. "Is he human now?" Another nod. "Was I his replacement from the start of it all?" Jordan looks at me for a long time before he nods again.

"So you send an Astro into the human world looking for children that have Lymerian ancestry? Then raise them until you can trick them into joining your race?" My hands are already gripping the chair in front of me tightly. With as much strength as I can gather, I swing the chair at the wall again and again until it breaks. The anger buried in the arena explodes from me. Behind closed doors I can do and say whatever I want.

In the silence that follows my outburst, I force my breathing to slow. I won't get information by attacking them. When he sees I've calmed somewhat, Jordan says, "It is not exactly like that." He pauses, making sure I won't throw anything else. "You have been his replacement since the day you were born." Suddenly I'm weak, my knees buckle beneath me. I hear all four of them reach for me, but Vic is there first. I wrap my arms around his neck and push my face against his shoulder, silently willing him to be my Vic again. His arms stay stiff below mine. He's holding me up, not holding on to me. His indifference to me hurts more than knowing my real parents were somehow part of this. I didn't know my parents, but I knew Vic. I love Vic, and he is breaking my heart.

"Give us a minute," Vic says to the others.

"No. I'm not leaving her alone with you."

"Two minutes, Kyle. He will not hurt her." It's an order and Kyle must follow, because it's true. Vic won't hurt me.

I hear them leave, my face is still buried in Vic's chest. He smells the same as before. Except my sense is stronger now, and I drown in him. I should have smelled him in the arena. The need to find Rebecca trumped my senses. That can't happen again.

"Please don't say it wasn't real," I whisper, still clinging to him. For ten years I thought I'd never see Vic or Rebecca again, and they are both here, with me, like me—forever. But it means nothing if Vic doesn't feel the same way, if we aren't friends or if we never were. Rebecca is here, but we are separated. Astros live on Mountain Top. So many nights I wished to be with them again. Not like this, a cruel joke that lasts an eternity.

"It was an assignment," Vic says flatly and gently detaches himself from me. I search his eyes, desperate for another flicker.

"Then why did you make them leave?"

"It is none of *their* business."

"It's not Clara's?" I challenge.

"The Guards."

He's lying. My emotions are calming down, and I can think with a clear head. We're still close, but I move in closer so that my lips are right next to his ear. I whisper, "I don't believe you. I still care about you very much, and I am a Guard. You know what that means. You don't get to lie to me."

Vic's heartbeat taps a little faster. "If you were Slayer, it would be different. But you are a Guard. Slayers and Guards cannot . . ."

"Can't be friends?"

"We cannot be family. I will be at court with the Slayers or where the Vegar sends me. Rebecca is on Mountain Top where she belongs. They are your family now." His words echo my last conversation with dream Vic in the cells below Krisenica. Not a dream.

"How did you find me down there? How did you . . . how did you get in the room? Why couldn't the others hear you? Or smell you? You were still you the first time you came." Vic tightens his jaw. What I've said doesn't confuse him. It was real. He was there. How?

"Rebecca helped me." I look around the room again, at the strange walls built uniquely to keep everyone out, even Astros. "Astros are talented beings. Rebecca is young, but truly gifted." I'd been so worried about Rebecca and how she was doing without me. It had all been in vain since Rebecca can take care of herself.

"But you came. The first chance you could, you found me," I say softly, slipping my arms around him again. He doesn't pull away.

"I made a mistake. I thought you would be a Slayer, because of Clara. Eventually Rebecca told me the truth." Heat flashes over me—not my emotions, but Vic's. He's angry, but I don't know why. Either because I'm not a Slayer, or because Rebecca waited to tell him. Maybe both.

His heat pulls back and I realize he is blocking me. "Two minutes is up." Vic jerks out of my arms and walks to the door.

"Please don't shut me out," I beg and reach for his arm. "Krisenica is small, and I will always feel your coldness." I don't want to be in pain like this forever.

"Do you want me to leave?" he asks harshly, his eyes begging me to give him a reason to go.

"No! I want you to stop doing this." I gesture at his whole body, his rigid stance. "Stop being this person that isn't you. Before you tell me that you were just playing a part, you didn't have to play *that* part. You didn't have to be this amazing person that made me need him. That made me love him. You were the greatest, Vic, you were . . ." My breath is heaving now, heart racing, but I don't care if he can hear it.

"You sound like a human. Do not do that out there." He points to the doors. "Being Lymerian means being a hundred times stronger than a human. That is what it takes to live thousands of years as I have, as Clara has. Live long enough and you will experience greater tragedies than a broken heart." Vic puts his hand on the door handle.

"You didn't answer my question," I say in a rush, refusing to let myself dwell on his words before I get my answers. "Why were you so wonderful?" I need to know so I can move on.

"Votaries are very important. We cannot afford to make mistakes with them. A relationship with Merrick was our main objective, but there was always a chance you would not like him." Vic starts to leave again, but stops. Lacking the courage to turn around, he adds in a bitter tone. "I worked very hard to make sure you liked me, but that is not who I am." The blood in my veins goes cold. Vic opens the door and leaves.

He's lying. The voice, the Guard that's been living inside me ever since I let go of my human self, knows the truth. I just don't know which part he's lying about. The others file back in and sit around the table. I let myself fall into the chair closest to the door.

"Did he make it clear he does not wish to see you?"

I glare at Clara. Everything I believed for the past fifteen years has been turned upside down on me, and she expects me to already accept it, to move on. Who am I if I was born to take someone's place? I was never going to have a human life. Does that make this easier or piss me off even more?

"You will do well to forget about Victor, Angelica. I have known him as long as I have known anyone. We are from the same surge and trained to be Slayers together. He is my second in command and will have no part of your life now that you are a Guard." If I believed anything she said, then her words might sting. I can feel myself going numb. "Now. It is time for me to tell you how Liturgy truly works."

"How can I trust anything you say, Clara?" Clara has managed to keep secrets from me for years—they all have. Will I know if she is lying now that I am sure of my Guard status?

"There is no higher law than Liturgy. We could not tell you about your birth until you completed your exams. *Once thy self be proven, the truth shall be free to you.*" I look at Clara, and there is not sadness or regret in her eyes. Jordan wears a face I've come to know well, unchanged and stern. Kyle won't meet my eyes. I reach for him with that other sense and feel his heartache. My caring for Vic has cut him deeply. He doesn't want me to love anyone but him.

When he feels my prodding, he cringes away. "Don't," he says, and I back off, too upset to be embarrassed at being caught.

Clara is waiting to tell her story. There is nowhere for me to go and no one but them to help me. Clara just said it—there is no higher law than Liturgy. I'm trapped here and there is nothing left for me to do but listen to whatever Clara wants to say to me.

Chapter 23

Clara

"What you know about Liturgy is true, but it is not the whole truth. For many years, Lymerians were allowed to leave at will and lead human lives. They married humans and had human children, aged and died. Our numbers decreased. Liturgy began.

"At first, with the help of Astros, we located humans with Lymerian ancestry. No one was forced to join, though many did. When are numbers stabilized, a compromise was forged between the Astros that wanted to give Lymerians the choice to be human and those that wanted to preserve our kind. Liturgy began. Becoming human would no longer come freely—you had to give something in return. All those that chose to become human must offer a replacement of their own blood. The first-born child of their first-born child must be returned to Lymerians to be the replacement for the next Lymerian in line to leave. Thus your debt is paid.

"Only human adults can survive the transition to Lymerian and sometimes even they do not. We had to find ways to keep the child in the human world but also remove them from their family at an early age. We have used stewards to raise and monitor the replacements for centuries. In addition to keeping an eye on the replacement, they are encouraged to form a bond. We have found the replacement embraces being Lymerian more quickly when they understand that they have not lost all their loved ones."

"The Franklins are my stewards," Angelica states wearily. I nod. "How are the stewards picked? Is it like Liturgy?"

"They volunteer."

She looks skeptical. "All of them volunteered? Even Vic? He volunteered to spend years with two Guards and a human?" The irony of our predicaments is not lost on me. Victor and I shared the same fate in this. "And what about Rebecca? Children volunteer? Is she even a child?"

"Victor volunteered because Merrick asked him to." At the mention of *his* name, Angelica tightens. "Stop," I say firmly and feel her pull whatever is about to come out back in. "Merrick is gone. If you want to waste time hating him for the rest of your life, you can, but that will not change the fact that he is gone. He is human now and under Lymerian protection. You are going to live long enough to see true cruelty. Merrick lied to you to get the life he wanted, but he followed our rules to get it. Your fate was sealed the moment you were born. If not Merrick, then another." She sets her jaw, grinding her teeth in fury.

"And Rebecca?" she growls.

"She is a young Astro, from Kyle's surge. If you saw a child when you looked at her, it is because she wanted you to see a child. She volunteered to be a steward because she knew it was her destiny to do so. That is what an Astro would say. Victor is telling the truth about her. She did take a risk helping you. She should never have left Mountain Top. There is a strong bond between you—now everyone knows that."

Relief waves over Angelica. Rebecca's kinship is real.

"Victor and Merrick are friends? Was Merrick a Slayer?" I nod. "They are both *your* Slayers?" She is accusing me because I am responsible for the choices my Slayers make. She has no idea how close she is to the real truth but for other reasons entirely.

"That is enough!" Jordan orders, rising to his feet. He glares at Angelica, silently chastising her implied accusation. Angelica does not flinch, but she looks hurt by Jordan's outburst. Kyle's head snaps up, obligated to defend Angelica under any circumstances. Jordan looks at Kyle. No one moves as the four of us stare at each other. "I think it is best if I wait outside," Jordan finally says.

"I'll go too." Kyle backs out of his chair, and they leave the room together. I pick up where we left off.

"Victor and Merrick were like brothers, inseparable since they were first born. Merrick wanted assurance with his chance to be human. He knew he could trust Victor, so Victor volunteered to be one of your stewards."

"What is Victor? What is a Tolken?"

"The Tolken is the second highest-ranking Slayer."

Angelica takes that in. Does she understand how unique a Guard she is? She has formed intimate relationships with the two highest-ranking Slayers, apart from Anubis. The scrolls weigh heavy in my mind. The decision to name Angelica Guard was not an easy one, but it is the right one. Denial or hiding her among Litmars cannot change what is.

It is hard to envision the Lymerian she will be someday. Angelica may carry this anger and sadness for lifetimes. It will mold her into someone who can lead us. But lead us where?

"Why all the games, Clara? Even if the stewards are necessary, why let me believe Merrick and me were real? Anyone could have stolen me in the night and brought me to you. I didn't need to fall in love."

"We could not steal you. We needed you to know what Merrick was and love him anyway. Furthermore, you had to understand how desperately he wanted to be human. Have you forgotten? Those moments that convinced you to give him your blood were real for him. Merrick wanted to be human more than anything. If we had taken you, you would not understand. You could not build trust. Without the bonds you formed with your stewards and the bonds you formed with us, you would not have survived."

Angelica looks away again. I can see something building in her, something she has been fighting off since the arena. Finally she looks at me, ready to ask the most important question. "Do you remember my grandparent?"

"I do not."

"How is that possible? All Lymerians must be present for ceremonies. Everyone saw Merrick, and they know what he's done." Angelica's eyes blaze with fury.

"Once the replacement is born and removed from their parents, the Astros block our memories of the Lymerian that is no more. Their commander, the Council, and a few others keep their memories. Since I was not their commander, my memories are gone."

"So Merrick will be erased someday? Everyone will forget him, even me?"

I shake my head. "You are his Replacement. You will remember him always."

Angelica ignites again, tearing the room apart. Once all the chairs and table are scattered and broken throughout the room, she sits on the floor, breathing hard.

Gently I take her hand. When I first told Angelica she was a replacement, I was overwhelmed with sorrow. That night I needed Jordan, and right now it should be Kyle holding her. But Kyle cannot hold her while she cries for the loss of another man.

"I thought he loved me." Angelica pulls her hand from mine so she can cover her face. Her shoulders shudder while she wastes her last tears on him. Merrick's infectious smile floods my barriers, forcing me to remember him one last time as well.

"Anyone would have fallen in love with Merrick." It is my only consolation since I cannot bring myself to wrap my arms around her. We are back in Krisenica, I am Vegar, and her sadness cannot touch me. Angelica and I must begin to grow apart. She is a Guard, and I am a Slayer.

She barely notices when I leave the room, consumed in her losses.

Outside the door, Kyle still looks like a wounded animal. Jordan stands emotionless as always.

"I leave her to you. Take her to our new quarters, and I will come later."

Jordan wants to ask me where I am going and why I am not coming with them, but he knows better. We are back in the real world now, and he cannot question me where others can hear him.

My first stop is the medic wing. Angelica severely wounded one of the Slayers, and I need to check in on her. Victor is already at Bree's bed. I take a deep breath to ready myself for this dance we must do. Bree is resting in a neck brace to ensure proper healing.

"How are you?"

"Vegar. I'll be fine." Bree is used to pain, but the neck injury is substantial. It will take weeks to heal depending on how much blood she accepts.

"You should not have taunted her. Angelica is my Votary, and you will respect her. Though she is Guard, she will be welcomed to the court by you and every other Slayer. Do you understand?" Bree is young and has not seen many Liturgies. No one is ready for a Votary they must respect, but she is my Votary. Bree nods. "Tolken, accompany me back to the court."

Victor stands and we walk side by side to the court. It has been decades since the two of us have been seen like this together. When we arrive, we head straight for one of the safe rooms. Like the giza, soundproof and Astro proof. He shuts the door and waits for me to speak first.

"What are you doing here? I ordered you to stay away." Victor's early return has created a ripple in everything I planned to do with Angelica. And he disobeyed an order, which Victor would only do on Anubis's behalf.

"Anubis sent for me, and he was right. She was too strong for them. Even if I had stayed away, nothing could have prevented Rebecca's interference. Angelica would have figured it out anyway." No matter how justified his reasons are, there must appear to be consequences. Victor understands that. Over the next weeks, he will play the part of repentant soldier.

Whether it was Anubis that made the decision or Etherial whispered in his ear, only the Tolken could have stood against Angelica. It was too dangerous for anyone else to try, and Bree was injured. Rebecca's involvement was the only thing that was going to push Angelica to her limits. Without her, Angelica would be with Farrell right now. Disgusted with that idea, I change the subject.

"How much has Rebecca told you about Angelica's future?" Victor looks at me, curious. "You are not her Guard, Victor. You are a Slayer. If you have an advantage with an Astro, then you are to use it to benefit us. Have you gone completely soft?" He has changed much since this all began, but he is still a Slayer. "Astros have many gifts, Victor. You knew the risk you took. I told you it would be unwise to volunteer."

Victor's face hardens. "I know about the Astros. Do you really think I would fall under her spell? Merrick has always been the fool, Clara, not me." I breathe deep. He knows exactly how to get under my skin. "It is not me you have worry about in regard to Rebecca—it is your Votary you must watch. Angelica's feelings for Rebecca are real."

"It is more than that. I need to know what Rebecca told you, Victor." Victor will tell me everything he knows. Not because I am his Vegar, but because he trusts me more than anyone else in Krisenica. The real question is how much did Rebecca let him remember.

"Rebecca is not like the other Astros. Futures come to her, but she does not seek them. Bits and pieces were all she ever told me. This Liturgy will be different. This Votary will be different. This Votary will be the strongest Lymerian yet to come."

Understanding washes over me. "And that is why you assumed Angelica would be Slayer. If you knew the truth, you never would have let yourself care for her."

Anger blazes in Victors eyes, not for me but what he has lost. In our lifetime, Victor has never had a mate. He has had companions, but never taken a mate. None of them were good enough for him.

"Why would Krisenica need a Guard that powerful?" Victor says as he starts to pace. "Ever since Rebecca told me that Angelica was a Guard, I have not been able to stop thinking about what that means." This reminds me of our many battles together, preparing plans before we strike.

"What have you concluded?" I ask slowly, speaking the words with meaning. I know the moment Victor comes to the same conclusion that Kyle, Jordan, and I came to years ago. He faces me, eyes wide with shock. The weight of the future of the Lymerian race sits between us.

"Remember that someday, you will have to choose a side."

Victor has a choice in this. My fate has already been written. Many nights I have laid awake preparing for what is to come. She is my Votary. I will never stand against her. Whomever is to be her ward has not yet tried to take power, but it is coming.

"Until then?" Victor asks, still holding my gaze.

"We change nothing. I shall not be the catalyst for what is to come. You have the Slayers. I will return when I can."

Victor nods once.

Chapter 24

Angelica

We leave the giza and walk for a long time, weaving through the tunnels and archways of Krisenica. Jordan leads, then me, and Kyle behind us. Between the two of them, I appear a well-protected prisoner. Am I a prisoner? No one explained the rules up here, only that we'd be together. The rest depended on my placement. *My placement.* The horror show in the arena replays, feeding oxygen to the small flame of fury that's been burning inside me since I recognized Vic's voice. I ignore the beautiful carvings in the walls, magnificent archways, and gawking onlookers, refusing to be distracted. Instead, I think about my options.

Two paths lie before me. Be Guard Angelica, Votary to the Vegar and mate to Kyle. Obey the laws of Krisenica. Forgive and forget everything that happened before the ceremony. Or wait, watch, and find a way to escape them as Merrick pretended to do. It's the first time I've dared to consider this possibility, but my performance in the arena gives me hope. Why should I stay? My Lymerian brain interrupts, asking the important questions. Is it even possible to outrun them? Where would I go? How could I hide from them?

Trumping every troubled thought is my trusted companion, the voice that dwells in the innermost part of me. *Rebecca. You must stay for Rebecca.*

Then what? Victor has abandoned me for his place with the Slayers. Rebecca is unreachable and an Astro. She doesn't need me—

Peter is her Guard. Can she even be trusted? Judy and Peter are Guards, but so what? They barely noticed me when we lived in the same house. The rest of the Lymerians are faceless beings. Clara told me once that I would find no friends in Krisenica. Kyle, Jordan, and Clara are all I have.

You have Rebecca. A hundred memories remind me why I can't leave.

We reach a long, high wall with a row of archways across the bottom. Kyle described this to me before, the entrance to the largest gymnasium. Guards live in gymnasiums, and I am a Guard. It looks like a maze of tunnels, each archway leading to a different path. Jordan doesn't pause as he guides us through several turns, eventually stopping in front of an opening—our new living quarters.

My room is modern, plaster walls and linoleum floors, but otherwise identical to my previous one. There is a light, chair, and bed, but also clothes. Now I shed my Votary red for Guard gray. Jordan and Kyle leave without saying anything to me. I listen to their footsteps, afraid of how far they will go from me. It's a silly thought. No matter how strained we are, Kyle is still my Guard. Both settle in nearby rooms, and I change.

It's hours before I track Clara moving toward us. Eventually she reaches our quarters and goes straight to her room. We stay divided in separate corners through the night. Liturgy pulls at us, whispers that we are stronger together. The sounds of the others shifting restlessly is a small consolation. I hope that their sleepless night has something to do with knowing how much they've hurt me. They are all liars. All Lymerians are liars.

Rebecca. She lied too, but she also risked something for me.

The past and the future run laps in my mind. Should I wholeheartedly accept my fate again? When I walked into the arena, I was ready to be one of them. But this, the depth of their lies, is too much. Yet there isn't another option. Even if I could leave Rebecca, an escape could take decades to plan. I'd have to play along and gain everyone's trust in the meantime. I'd never be able to fool Clara.

The past steps in, flaunting Merrick and our fake romance. Once cherished memories turn to bile in my throat. I truly thought he loved me, and I was stupid enough to love him, to want to spend a lifetime with him. Now I hate him. Clara knew the whole time and let me cry for him anyway.

She told as much truth as she could, the Guard voice whispers.

Maybe. That doesn't mean I forgive her.

I want to find Merrick. I want him to confess to his sins, to admit that his life was worth more than mine. And what about his unborn grandchild? He desperately wanted children yet is willing to give one up for the price of his freedom, just like my grandparent did.

My head hurts, my *heart* hurts. I take my grief and hatred for Merrick and bury it. If Clara is right, I will remember Merrick, and someday he will answer to me. Right now, I have to move on, starting with Kyle.

A few years ago, I wandered into his room, and he let me in. This time there's no welcome—just the wall he's put up around himself. He doesn't want excuses for what I feel. Kyle wants to run away from everything, from me. Liturgy has given me many things, but they come with a price. If I want Kyle's protection and love, I have to completely let go of Vic and my human life.

I hesitate at the opening to Kyle's room. He is lying on his bed, staring at his ceiling. "Can I come in?"

When he doesn't answer, I start to leave.

"Jordan loved Clara from the beginning of all this. Maybe he never stopped loving her from when they were young, just buried it until you walked into the arena. I jumped into it blindly too. It's how I've been my whole life. I jump first and ask questions later." Kyle stops looking at the ceiling and turns his gaze to me. "I loved you from the moment I laid eyes on you. When you were still human." My heart drops. His pain is so real and runs deep. I can feel it pulsing from across the room. "You love them both," he says, his reddened eyes turning back at the ceiling.

"I don't love Merrick," I say, hardening. "I hate Merrick." And if I ever see him again, I'll try to tear him apart.

Kyle looks at me again, trying to decide if I really mean that.

"Kyle, I was seventeen when I met Merrick, and human. Ten years isn't very long for you, but until yesterday I thought I moved on." I take a deep breath and force myself to stop the train of emotions demanding to come out. *It's done*, my inner voice assures me.

"Tolken," he says, unmoved. "I saw you with him. You want him to be your Guard, to protect you and care for you like he used to."

There isn't an easy answer to defend how I feel about Vic, but I'm not going to lie to Kyle like everyone has lied to me.

"Kyle, consider how I feel after today. My only friends lied to me. And I know you all think it's for the right reasons, but you broke my heart. You broke my heart much worse than Merrick did. Merrick used me and lied to me for a year. You lied to me for ten years. Maybe you didn't know me during those first years, but you knew me much longer than Merrick did."

Kyle sits up. The anger in his eyes a minute ago is gone, but I'm not done.

"I guess I thought that I could find the Vic I'd known before. But that person isn't real either. It's as if we are starting over; everyone is a stranger. The only sure thing is how you feel about me, and I need you on my side."

For a moment, Kyle doesn't move, and I worry he's abandoned me like Vic. Then he walks, slowly, across the room. He puts his arms around me. Instead of crying because I feel safe, I take his strength and make it my own.

"I'll always protect you, Angelica." I can feel his voice rumbling from his chest against my cheek. "But it can't be like it was in the dungeons. Not for a long time."

I look up and remember the time we lost ourselves in a kiss. His eyes tell me he is far from wanting to kiss me again.

"Isaac wants to see you." Clara's speaking from the doorway. Kyle pulls away and walks out the door.

The hallways are narrow in the gymnasium, forcing us to walk in a single line at times. As we go deeper, I realize how out of place Clara is, covered in black. The three of us are Guards and with our division—she is the outsider now. There hallways are infinite, one never-ending maze. In the center, Isaac waits.

Guards begin to appear as we make our way deeper. Some of them are in their rooms reading, writing, sleeping, or isolated in concentration. Larger rooms hold more Guards engaged in a common activity, some playing chess.

As I'm warming to the idea of playing chess again, a chill tingles my spine. It's Clara I'm picking up on. She has gone ice cold. Clara and Jordan are far behind Kyle and me. We backtrack and a tall, dark-haired woman is looming over Clara. Her body is stiff, fingers rigid at her sides with a glare that could kill fixed on Clara. I let my Guard sense taste the charge between the three of them and suck in a breath, immediately reeling it back.

"Slayers are not allowed here," she growls. Clara is steel, concealing all traces of her love for Jordan. I'm itching to do something, but I'm an outsider. Nearby Guards stop what they are doing. Kyle stiffens, reacting to my uneasiness. I can almost hear him screaming in my head, *Votaries do not fight their Architect's battles, especially the Vegar's.* He knows my Guard instinct will push me to protect anyone I care about, especially Clara.

"Karina, how many Guards do you think it would take to make me leave?"

Karina is silent. Clara swings her gaze to me then back to Karina.

"Actually, I need not fight at all. If you touch me, none here can stop her."

She is right. Despite everything, I would risk my life for her. For the first time, I understand what it means when Clara says there is no higher law than Liturgy.

"Who are you?" I ask, stepping toward the woman. Kyle doesn't try to stop me, but he stays very close. Karina and I are the same height, forcing our eyes to lock. She doesn't know what to do. I haven't done anything to her and whether she likes it or not, I'm a Guard too. Almost on instinct, I reach my mind out to her but pull back a second later. It's all I need to know the story. This woman is broken, much more broken than me, and it is Clara's fault. Her heartache makes mine seem like child's play.

"None of us asked for this, Karina," I say and turn around to keep walking. Kyle, Clara, and Jordan follow. Karina doesn't respond, and it's over just like that.

Isaac is in a large circular room with golden walls climbing far higher than the dungeon cell. They must reach to the top of the mountain. The walls are perforated and hold thousands of scrolls of paper, each tied precisely with red twine.

"Assignments, past, present, and future," Isaac says in a deep voice that is naturally amplified and authoritative. "The Astros protect them so that only I can remove or add scrolls. As you might imagine, I spend a lot of time in here." Isaac is massive, taller than Kyle and Jordan. He is far older than Clara, yet more human. Most of the Guards I've seen look human-ish, which implies contact with humans. *Or they drink human blood.*

"Clara," Isaac continues, silencing my inner Guard. "I never imagined you in one of my gymnasiums. It is good to see you." Isaac sounds sincere and completely unafraid of her.

Clara nods. She respects him too. "There are more tunnels than I imagined." She doesn't return his smile.

"It is good for training." Isaac turns away from Clara. "Jordan, Kyle, you have brought great honor to the Guards." Both Jordan and Kyle nod. Part of me wants to reach out to Isaac to see behind the mask of sincerity. I doubt he would appreciate that. "Kyle, Angelica, take a seat and we will begin." Jordan and Clara don't seem like they mind being left out. Is this the plan? We take our seats.

"Angelica, let me properly introduce myself. I am Isaac, commander of the Guards and of the first born here on Earth. You may have noticed, I look a bit older than the faces you are used to seeing." He pauses, maybe waiting for me to smile. I don't. "A lot of the Vegar in you I see. Your examination was breathtaking, unlike anything I have ever seen. Never has Guard defeated two Slayers, and you bested three. And the Tolken—you stood your own ground against him. Impressive."

"Thank you," I say when it seems like Isaac is finished with his speech. "You can thank Clara."

Isaac looks over my shoulder to Clara, but his expression stays the same. He never doubted a Votary of Clara's would be a force.

"We move now into a different part of Liturgy. The four of you can continue living together on the edge of the Guard quarters for as long as you like. Over time, it will be natural for you to rely less on your Architect and more on your division. When you are ready, you and Kyle will move into the regular living quarters for Guards."

Several emotions explode in me, but I'm getting good at hiding them from those who don't know me well. I'm sure Clara and maybe Kyle senses my unrest. For his sake, I hope Kyle cannot. Physically I stay calm, but my mind starts to panic. Isaac is talking like the rest of eternity has been written. Me and Kyle and the Guards while Clara just fades away. I'm not ready to lose her.

"I think that will be all for today," Clara says, coming to my rescue. Kyle and I rise, quick to obey. Isaac notices Kyle's abrupt response, and his masks slips for less than a heartbeat. No one sees but me. A mixture of pride, fear, and arrogance stir in me until a look from Isaac squashes it. Oops.

"We should start right away. Angelica, would you like a tour of your new home?" Jordan is on point, ushering us gracefully from Isaac's quarters.

Jordan's first stop is a series of training rooms. Every room I see has at least two doors, so it is impossible to guess where the gymnasiums end.

"This place really is a maze. Do you know every inch of it?"

Jordan nods. "The paths serve many functions. Some of it has to do with training, being able to test our tracking abilities. Most of it is about keeping our wards safe when necessary."

"Why do Lymerians need protection?" I've been wondering for a while now. Why do Slayers and Guards train so much? What do they think is coming?

"Humans," Clara says and steps into the room. "And others in the universe. In the beginning, we guarded ourselves because we thought it probable other races would try to come to this perfect planet. We wanted to be able to protect ourselves, should they come."

"Have others come?" It's hard to imagine more space people coming here, but the Lymerians exist, so why not.

"Yes. And they will come again. Our training is endless because the threat is endless. We have seen the unbelievable." I want to hear more about what they have seen over the centuries, but Clara is not in the mood.

"What about humans? What threat are they?"

Clara snickers, liking this subject better. "When we came here, humans worshiped many gods and fought with spears. They were no match for us. We thought they were weak. Over time we have seen their strength and will. Their technology continues to advance, and soon they shall have the means to eradicate our entire race if they chose to."

"Why would they?" The Lymerians live in secret and go to great lengths to stay hidden.

"If humans discover what the Astros can do, then they will stop at nothing to enslave them." I want to argue, to defend humans. But I grew up in the aftermath of the worst war in human history. Humans are capable of driving a race to extinction.

I remember the hooded figures in the arena during my examination. Not enough to stand against the human race. Liturgy and surges are necessary for their sanity and survival. They can't risk a Slayer going crazy from thousands of years of living, but they can't just let them become human without . . . a replacement. There has to be a better way.

Jordan picks up where Clara left off. "That is why we built these labyrinths throughout Krisenica. The Astros live safely on Mountain Top, but should we be attacked, they are to locate their Guard or Guards and evacuate Krisenica while the Slayers hold off the invaders."

"But I thought the Astros could see, well, everything?"

Kyle, Jordan, and Clara are silent. None of them has an answer.

"Whatever it is they see, they want it this way," Kyle says dismissively, and Clara gapes at him as if seeing him for the first time. From our lessons, I know Clara has complete faith in the Astros though not everyone in Krisenica shares her belief. Especially the younger Lymerians. She didn't realize where Kyle stood with the Astros. I thought it was obvious how he felt.

Jordan walks ahead. "We should move on."

Chapter 25

Angelica

Year one as a Guard ticks by on Lymerian time. Life above ground is demanding, molding what's left of my human bits into solid Lymerian. The betrayals of Liturgy continue to live within me though my heart has calmed. I'm learning to be a Guard, pushing my instincts past their limits again and again. Every day they are stronger, whispering secrets and guiding my actions. They tell me who deserves forgiveness, empathy, and hatred.

Vic's and Rebecca's lies are less traumatizing now that I've learned to trust the Guard inside me. *They weren't always pretending*, it soothes. *Rebecca left Mountain Top to be in the arena with you. Vic is lying.*

There is, however, one villain in my story, a person I can't forgive—Merrick. Clara says that if not Merrick then another, but my instincts tell me that isn't true. Liturgy ceremonies have decreased over time, which means more Lymerians are choosing to stay Lymerian. No matter how hard I try, I can't stop reliving the year we spent together and how hard he worked to get my love. I loved him enough to die for him, and I was nothing to him—a means to an end. That pain just won't fade.

Most of the year I spend with Kyle. He shows me all the gymnasiums in Krisenica. I learn their tunnels and secrets. The Lymerians say there are four gymnasiums, but they are all connected. We make a game of hide-and-seek. He hides, and I seek. Both of us know it's training for me, but it's still fun. When I finally reach him, I feel good that my instincts are spot on and happy to be with him again. *His love is eternal.*

Somewhere in those tunnels, I start to love him like I did before we left the dungeons. Sometimes it feels like a future with him could be a content one. While we spend many days moving through the gymnasiums, I don't get to leave them. For whatever reasons, they are keeping me isolated with the Guards.

Most of the Guards are couples sharing quarters. Some have been together for hundreds of years. Karina was Jordan's mate and now everything has changed for them. The torment I felt from her was the result of breaking a deep bond. We haven't seen her since the first day. Kyle says she asked Isaac for an assignment in the human world.

Everyone assumes Kyle and I are mates, but he treats me more like a sister, always holding himself back. He has many friends in our division, and they welcome me. He isn't as lighthearted as before but definitely isn't like the rest of the Guards. I can feel their swarms of emotions, but they don't laugh or cheer when they play games. They mask their emotions like Jordan.

When I'm not running the tunnels with Kyle, Clara and I train. Her knowledge of combat is endless. The rest of Clara's time is spent with the Slayers in the court. *Let her be with her Slayers. She will always come back to you.* Everyone agrees that I shouldn't go to the court. I don't argue, because I don't want to see Vic. I know both he and Rebecca are still in Krisenica. When it's late at night and Krisenica is quiet, I reach for them.

My emotional connection with them makes tracking easy, though Rebecca is harder for me to reach than Vic. I'm not sure what Mountain Top is, but I think it is farther away than anyone realizes. Anyone that doesn't have an Astro for a ward. Vic is everywhere. He moves through all the wings of Krisenica except the gymnasiums. Maybe he thinks he's doing me a favor by avoiding me. Sometimes I stay up for hours tracking him, part of me hoping he will make the turn into my gymnasium. But he never does.

Jordan spends most of his time with Isaac. *Honor, duty, loyalty, trust him.* I know because I track him. Jordan still finds time to work with me and insists I keep focusing on this specific skill. He says I should be able to track anyone, not just the people I'm close to. Finally, I understand what all the Guards are doing when they sit with their eyes closed. They are our best trackers, pushing themselves beyond what they could do the day before.

Isaac occupies my thoughts as well. He rarely asks for me, but I hope that changes. If my grandfather or grandmother was a Guard, then Isaac remembers them. Are they still alive? Can they lead me to my parents? After understanding Janice's loss, I felt blessed to be rid of uncertain memories, but now I want them back.

As this first year reaches its conclusion, I catch a glimpse of how powerful Clara truly is among Lymerians. She changes history before my eyes.

"I do not understand why I cannot ask them if they want to join us." We are training and Clara wants to invite the Guards nearby.

"Did you ask Isaac?"

Clara glares at Jordan. Even if it is Isaac, Vegars don't ask. Hasn't he learned that yet?

I come to Jordan's rescue, which earns me the same look from Clara. "He is the commander of the Guards, Clara. Be realistic."

"I'm sure Clara would just love someone to start training with her Slayers," Kyle adds, really putting her in her place. I have to turn my face to hide a smile.

"That is entirely different," Clara growls back. "Why are you suddenly so concerned with what Isaac thinks?" Hasn't she noticed how much time Jordan spends with him? Ignoring all of us, Clara walks into the nearest training room occupied by three Guards.

"Silas, Marie, Aaron, would you join us in some exercises?" It was sort of a question, I guess, but none of them are going to tell her no. All six of us gape at Clara. The Guards seem more shocked that the Vegar knows their names than at the invitation to train.

"Let us begin. I will not draw blood, I promise. Kyle and Jordan are getting a bit rusty, and they refuse to combat against Angelica or myself. Take turns sparring."

The three Guards move, and it begins.

A group of Guards soon fall under her training. Not all the Guards, but she doesn't turn anyone away. Even among Guards, Clara is who she is. Maybe that's why Isaac lets her keep doing it. Or maybe he thinks his Guards could use the instruction. Either way, Jordan says he has never seen anything like it happen between divisions. I marvel at Clara. She is more than the other Lymerians.

* * *

Clara dedicates more time to my training during Guard year two and drives me twice as hard. Sometimes it's just us, other times we work with Guards. I no longer have to worry about how to fight multiple opponents. They flock to us, enamored by the Guard Clara has created, wanting to be just as strong.

Without wards, it comes down to skill. Clara wants my skills to be impeccable, so when I'm fueled by the need to protect, no one can stop me. I don't know what she thinks is coming or who my ward might be, but she is relentless in training. My clothes are nearly always stained in blood, either mine or my opponent's. With their consent, we now draw blood.

As I spend more time with Clara, Kyle spends more time away from our quarters. Our games of hide-and-seek dwindle until there are none at all. One night after training, I seek him without permission. This time I don't need tracking. All I have to do is follow the sound of laughter. Guards don't laugh like that unless he's around. I find him with a group of Guards in one of the game rooms.

"Do you want to play chess?" I ask him, noticing the chess board as I walk in to the room.

"You know I read your transcripts from year four. Chess is your game with the Tolken."

I close my eyes and breathe. How could he mention Vic in front of these Guards? What do I do now? Walk out of the room? *Don't give up.* "Does anyone want to play?"

The others refuse to meet my eyes. Clara said this would happen. The Guards have been nice to me because of Kyle. To them, I'm just a Votary. If Kyle turns on me, so will they. None of these Guards train with Clara, which might be why Kyle chose them. Regardless, I'll find no allies here. I leave the room.

An hour later, Kyle is standing in the doorway to my room. He knows I've been sitting here alone, rejected. My emotions are tied to his as long as he is my Guard. Why is he hurting me? *Because he's hurting.*

"Don't," I say as Kyle moves to step in the room. Kyle sighs and leans against the doorframe.

"We've been up here for two years, and you've barely touched me," he says quietly.

Before I let myself react, I reach for Jordan and Clara. They aren't close enough to interrupt or overhear this conversation. None of the other Guards will come this way; it's safe to talk. Clara's Vegar habits are rubbing off on me.

"You said it wasn't going to be like the dungeons. I've been waiting for you to . . ." I don't know what to say. He is completely different toward me than he was in the dungeons. Somehow, I thought I'd know when he was ready.

"Me? After how you reacted to Isaac's assumption of us?" Shame fills me as I remember the panic that threatened to consume me when Isaac presumed Kyle and I were going to be forever. I had hoped my emotions were under control. Clara had known how I felt; Kyle did too.

"That was right after the exams. You know—"

"I know!" Kyle shouts, cutting me off. We stare at each other as unwelcome memories threaten to reopen healing wounds. Our emotions turn at the same time, anger and hurt replaced by passion. We meet in the middle of my room, our lips coming together so forcefully that Kyle's lip splits.

Kyle backs away. "I'm sorry."

"Don't be." I step to him and wrap my arms around his waist. Tension melts from my limbs as his arms enclose me. We stay joined minute after minute, until every piece of us is reconnected. He breaks away first, taking my face in his hands and kissing me gently. I lick the crusted blood on his lips until I can suppress my hunger no long.

In a flash, my creese is across his neck, lips tugging gently in rhythm with his pulse. The blood feels hot, and the passion in me soars again. Kyle's self-control breaks, and he jerks my wrist to his lips. Not bothering with a creese, he bites down and drinks from me. I shiver as tiny shards of my soul become part of him. In return, I receive his love, loyalty and undying devotion. I gasp and pull away.

"I'm so sorry," Kyle whispers.

"For what? That was amazing." Merrick's method for blood taking was formal, *civilized* he called it. Needles, alcohol swabs, and band aids were necessary tools. To think we could have been doing this, would have been doing this, if ever loved me.

"Exchanging blood is . . . something mates do when both of them are ready."

"I was ready."

"No, you weren't." I open my mouth to protest but clamp it shut when I see his sorrow. "Do you remember our lessons on blood exchange?" The last bit of warmth from our kiss slips away. "You still love him." My eyes soften, ready to back up the lie forming between my lips, but Kyle shakes his head, chastising me. We have no secrets now. Blood doesn't lie. "I'm not giving up on you, but I'm not all in yet."

* * *

A few months later, Kyle and I are playing one of our seeking games when I feel a pull in another direction. Instead of looking for Kyle, I move away toward something that feels like a memory. It doesn't take me long to find them. Peter and Judy are surprised to see me, which means they've been avoiding me.

It's easy to see that they are mates in real life and volunteered to be my stewards together. I can tell by the way Peter steps slightly in front of Judy when our eyes meet. He is getting ready to protect her in case I hold a grudge against them.

"Angelica," Peter says. "We saw you in the arena during your examinations."

"We've never seen anything like it," Judy adds. Her tone reminds me of the memory I had in my dreams, when I overheard a few people talking in the dining room. It must have been Vic, Judy and Peter.

"It was very surprising. We were certain you would be a Slayer. You and Vic—I mean the Tolken, got along so well." Peter cuts himself off as Kyle rounds the hallway to join us. The three nod to each other. If Kyle were not here, I would ask Peter if Vic was acting with me. I wish I could let it go. Instead I gather myself.

"I'm glad I ran into you. Thank you for everything," I say, remembering that I represent Clara at all times. Judy smiles and we part ways, understanding our time together is over. I was not close to Peter and Judy in the human world; it doesn't make sense to try and change that now.

* * *

"Angelica, could you come here please." Isaac's voice is as clear as if he were standing next to me. I spin around, searching for him. Kyle jumps up, trying to find the danger. He didn't hear anything—Isaac is in my head.

"I need to go see Isaac," I tell Kyle. He stands up to join me, but I tell him he should stay.

I close my eyes and think of Isaac, because I know he wants me to find him. Heading to his office would be too obvious. If he wanted to make it easy, he would have showed up at my quarters. First, I need to leave this room. I can't concentrate with Kyle watching me.

Once I get a good distance away from Kyle, I stop and listen. There isn't anyone around. I close my eyes again and think about Isaac, what he feels like. Isaac is the oldest and probably strongest of the Guards not on the Council. He shouldn't be hard to find, but I'm getting nothing. Even my inner Guard is quiet. Suddenly, I figure out another way. I can't find Isaac, but I can find Jordan.

This time when I close my eyes, it only takes a few seconds for me to catch up to where Jordan is. They are on the move, not very fair in a game of hide and seek. It takes me about ten minutes to reach where they are in the west gymnasium. Jordan is surprised to see me, especially without Kyle. Isaac's expression tells me nothing.

"Angelica, let us find somewhere private to talk. Jordan, I will see you tomorrow." Jordan nods and walks away without giving me a second look. I follow Isaac into a small room with a door. Doors are rare in Krisenica. The walls aren't Astro proof, but I guess nothing in the gymnasiums can be.

"You have been a Guard for almost three years. It is time to make some changes." He must want Kyle and me to move fully into the Guard quarters. What will Jordan and Clara do? They will be parted.

"Have you talked to Clara?" I ask because it seems like he should talk to Clara first. This is still Liturgy. I wonder when it stops being Liturgy. *Soon.*

"Yes."

"What is going to change?"

"Clara and I agree that you have far too much potential to train with ordinary Guards. You will continue your Guard training, but with me instead of Kyle and Jordan. Your combat training will continue with Clara, both in the gymnasiums and the court."

Again, my mind responds before my body so I can keep my focus. I tell myself I will worry about Vic and the Slayers when I am alone. "What about our living arrangements?"

"That is none of my concern. You, Kyle, Clara, and Jordan can decide what will work best with the change in training."

Isaac waits for me to ask another question. I am full of them, but now isn't the right time to bring up the past. *Patience.* He is going to train me. There will be other opportunities.

"Another thing. Come here." I walk closer to him. He takes my right hand in his, like we are shaking hands. "You have to be able to seek those you do not care about. Physical contact will help you. Touch as many people as you can."

I close my eyes and reach for him. He's right—it's easier to find him when we are touching. Isaac is able to let me in without letting me go into his essence. A thousand things distinguish Isaac from other Lymerians. I'd guess every Lymerian is unique in this way—

humans too, and all life on Earth. After several minutes, he drops my hand.

"Did you get enough?" I nod. "Remember, Angelica, the mind is like any other part of our bodies. It will not go beyond itself until you show it that it must."

"Do all Guards have the potential to go into someone's mind?" I don't know why, but I want to learn his trick. It's something Clara can't teach me.

"If a Guard is exceptionally talented, they will be able to communicate with their ward telepathically."

"I'm not your ward."

"No. You are the Vegar's Votary. Since the moment Clara stepped forward during the ceremony, I have been preparing to train a Guard of strength like we have never seen. These past thirteen years, I have been pushing my mind everyday beyond its limits to prepare for you."

This truth hits me deeper than the others. Clara is my Architect, and that truth tells me I will match her in many ways once my training is complete. Isaac's truth tells me others are preparing themselves for what that could mean for the Lymerians. I want to ask so much more, but he gestures, a signal that we are done for today.

I think about Isaac's words on the way back to my room. He can talk to me in my mind because he trained himself to do it. Clara pushes her body to the extreme and Isaac pushes his mind. Commanders are the best of the Lymerians because they continue to push far beyond what the other Lymerians are willing to do. How do I fit into that? What is my purpose here?

Chapter 26

Clara

"It has been months since Isaac began working with Angelica," Jordan says as he caresses my arm. We are deep within the mountains that surround Krisenica. Several times a year we come out here and hide ourselves, spending hours alone. Our divisions never see us touch or smile at each other, but they know Karina's departure can only mean that Jordan has no intention of going back to her. Still, it must be this way. The Vegar cannot show passion for anything but her Slayers and now, her Votary.

"And?" I ask, taking a moment to kiss him before he can go on.

"Move back to the court. It is time—you know that." I do, but I needed him to say it first. I kiss him again. This time I bite his lip and draw blood. Tasting your lover's blood is the highest form of closeness that Lymerians share. We did not exchange in the dungeons. Only when in the safety of these secluded woods did we dare and only small amounts.

"I will leave tonight."

Jordan kisses me this time, biting hard. "What will you tell Angelica?"

Nearly four years have passed since her placement and the understanding that everything she has ever known is a lie. She and Victor have not crossed paths since, but she notices when I train with him. Every time I see her after I have been close to him, her demeanor changes instantly. Part of her is angry at him still, but another part is jealous that I get to be with him. When I leave the gymnasiums, it will become necessary for her to spend time at the court. They cannot avoid each other forever.

"Angelica is expecting it. If anything, she will be relieved." It is better to face the dread than dread the day. "It is Kyle I worry about. He will be incredibly unhappy every time she goes to the court. The moment he catches Victor's scent on her, it will drive a wedge between them."

Jordan pulls away, begins to speak then changes his mind. I glimpse the fading sun on the horizon, a sign we have been gone too long. We reach for our things.

"She will never be *his* mate," Jordan finally says. It is rare for him to vocalize this kind of cruel logic. I abandon the effort of getting dressed and kiss him again.

"They have exchanged blood, Jordan, more than once."

"And yet she has not taken him for a mate, not even to her bed. She is afraid to lose him, yet cannot commit."

I nod thoughtfully. "He did not give her a fair choice, and he will face those consequences someday. I would rather not be caught in the path of his jealousy. He has quite a temper."

"I love the dark in you," Jordan says, ending the discussion and kissing me one more time. "I love how it spills into every piece of you. From your beautiful eyes and gorgeous black hair to the coldness that surrounds your heart." Jordan takes my face in his hands and looks straight into my eyes. "I have *always* loved it about you. You are the only person that lets me be who I really am instead of who everyone else needs me to be."

"I love you too."

It is all I have air to say—he has taken my breath away.

* * *

"To what do I owe a visit from the Vegar?" Isaac asks when he finds me waiting for him in his office a few days later.

“I am moving back to the court.” I tell Isaac as a courtesy. As commander of the Guards, he should be informed of living changes in the gymnasiums.

“Ah. That explains Jordan’s poor mood following your last rendezvous.” I am impressed with Isaac. Jordan is quite good at disguising his feelings, especially in front of Isaac, yet Isaac noticed.

“Also, it is time for Angelica to further explore Krisenica.”

“With you,” he states more than asks.

“Of course,” I reply.

“I have seen many Liturgies, Clara. She is more Lymerian than most of us. The others do not treat her as they have treated Votaries in the past.”

“That is because Kyle is well liked. It will not be the same outside of your gymnasiums.”

“True. You as her Architect will help her win some Slayers, but not all. We saw the resentment certain Slayers have for her during the examination. You give her what they want most—personal attention and training. Yet she is not a Slayer. They do not understand why you continue to train her.”

I think Isaac is searching for information, anything that will help him understand how Angelica fits into our world. Perhaps he knows more than he is letting on. I do not know if I can trust Isaac, but he is Angelica’s commander. I need to know where he stands with Farrell.

“You sound as if you have been speaking to Farrell.” I cannot help the icy tone that comes when I say his name.

“It is smart politics to maintain good relationships with the other commanders, the Council, and key division members. Your Tolken understands that.” Now Isaac really sounds like Farrell. Not the right move.

“Exactly. He is the Tolken and not the Vegar, or have you forgotten?” I pause, hoping he recalls my moment of triumph as clearly as I do. “It is obvious you maintain a good relationship with Farrell. You should know there is none that I trust more than the Tolken and Jordan. No matter how much time you spend with either of them, they will never tell you what you want to know unless I say they can." I do not know what Isaac wants, but he should have simply asked. Instead he plays mind games.

"In regard to my Votary, I will address your inquiry because she is your Guard. Whatever powers there are behind Liturgy, they gave Angelica me for an Architect. They want her to be as disciplined as I am. You will teach her many things that I cannot, but you cannot teach her how to slay." I stand to leave. We are done here.

"Are you teaching my Guards to Slay?" Isaac knows why we train with Guards.

"Soon enough I shall be out of your gymnasiums for good." He smiles and I pivot to the door.

"When will you release Jordan?" Isaac asks in a much different tone. He does not like a Guard beholden to the Vegar, especially a Guard as strong as Jordan. With my back to him, I let myself smile.

"I released Jordan years ago. The Vegar does not need a Guard." Isaac is silent, so I leave to collect my things.

Kyle and Angelica are not in our area of the gymnasium when I stop to gather the few things I keep here. Alone, I let myself remember the past fourteen years. In my mind, each scene flashes by in mere moments. I did not want this, but I far from regret it. The agony of losing each of my children will forever stain red a corner of my darkened heart.

Somehow, I have been given a child that I never need give up. We will spend lifetimes together, and it is all because of Merrick. What he could not give me in life, he gave me in his death.

* * *

"Angelica," I say, standing at the edge of her gymnasium. Our connection is still strong, allowing me to call to her mind over short distances. This is necessary to ensure we do not encounter Kyle. Today I am taking Angelica to the court for the first time, and Kyle cannot be near us. Now that Angelica and Kyle are no longer spending every moment together, I can sneak her away. Jordan agreed to keep Kyle busy so that neither Angelica or I had to tell him what we are doing. Kyle will find out, but we save the fight for after the session. Angelica cannot walk into the Slayer's den after arguing with Kyle.

"You're taking me to the court today." Angelica is already by my side. Next to me she is substantial and will walk into the court looking the part. Her muscles bulge slightly under her gray division clothing. Combined with her height, she looks like a true Guard. Why am I surprised? I have known her path for years. "Jordan and Kyle never hang out. I figured something was happening, and there's only one thing you'd want to do that Kyle wouldn't like."

"We can put it off no longer."

"Why do I need to go there? The other Guards have never set foot at the court."

Angelica whispers this to me, all too aware that someone is usually listening in Krisenica. Nearly fifteen years have gone by and still I hold back. After the exams, can I admit to more lies? How can I tell her who she is and who Merrick was? I ignore her question.

"This is exactly the way you behaved when it was time to leave your cell. Stop acting out. We are going now."

Angelica immediately hardens her expression, gaining the upper hand over her emotions. She knows I am right. It is unrealistic that she will never see Victor again. Facing him will make her stronger.

"Did you tell him?" she asks quietly, keeping her head up. We are walking shoulder to shoulder, eyes scanning every inch of our surroundings.

"No. That would be absurd, Angelica. Please imagine this from the perspective of someone that has lived thousands of years."

Angelica stiffens again, fighting to stay completely calm. I stop in front of a void.

"Through there?" She nods to the entrance of the Slayer's division. "It looks like a black cave."

"We like the dark," I say and start walking again before she gets more worked up. We are not far in when her heart beat changes. I stop and stare at her. It is too late to use words to console her. Instead I stare deep in her eyes and shake my head once. *No.* She will keep herself calm in front of my Slayers. Angelica breathes, and we keep moving.

"What is that light ahead?"
"The court."
"It's white? I thought you liked the dark."
"The court is different. Before we reach the court, there will be a series of rooms we use to strategize. All of them are soundproof. A few of them are unreachable." Slayers like their privacy. The Slayers wing has more doors than the rest of Krisenica combined. "Beyond the court are our living quarters."
"It's beautiful," Angelica says as we walk into the court. Before she can finish, the court goes silent. The word "beautiful" carries through the high ceiling.
"Continue," I say softly and the room fills once again with commotion. Three Slayers break from their training and walk over to us.
"Vegar, will you allow your Votary to train with us?"
I scan them carefully, remembering Isaac's prediction. Is this invitation a sign of respect, an attempt to push Angelica around, or do they want a good fight? No matter what their intentions are, my answer must be yes.
"I've been told broken necks take longer to heal than you'd think. Broken backs are worse," Angelica replies before I can give any of them an answer. She is . . . protecting me. Her fears and worries are of no consequence as she puts my needs in front of hers. Angelica knows she is my Votary, and that means showing no fear in front of my Slayers.
"How many would you like Angelica?" This is her fight; she should decide the path it takes.
"How many Slayers can you do without?" she asks. Kyle's humor is rubbing off on her.
"You are confident for a Guard without a ward. A Guard is at their strongest when they are fighting in defense of someone else," Skylar, my most promising Slayer from the last surge, says as he joins the other three.
"She is fighting for something," Victor says from across the room. His appearance takes everyone by surprise except Angelica. She knew where he would be the moment I called her out of the

gymnasium. This explains her earlier reservations. “Angelica has spent fifteen years training with our Vegar. Now it is her chance to show us what she has learned. Trust me, Slayers, she will not lose today.”

It begins. Victor and I move to the side as the four Slayers spread out. They dance around her, taking quick hits. All are exceptional Slayers. Their plan of attack is to wear her down while conserving their energy. This dance will become faster and faster, but unlike your average Guard, Angelica will not wait to attack. She will attack when she finds an opening. It will be fast, strong, and they will all fall.

The rest of the Slayers stop their exercises and fill out around the fight, watching. Benjamin comes behind her and tries to hold her arms down while the other Slayers attack. Angelica immediately kneels and jumps backward. Benjamin’s back takes the brunt of the fall as they hit the ground. Before he can move, she presses her shoulders back and puts all her strength into hitting him again. Benjamin is done, his rib cage crushed.

“That is good,” Victor says and the others stop their advance. “I think we know how the rest will play out.” Victor leans over Benjamin and examines him. “Never underestimate the strength of a Guard, Benjamin, especially when they have something to fight for.”

“Show us how to fight her,” Skylar says. Victor stands and looks at Angelica. Her eyes are unreadable, even for me.

“I did show you,” Victor says, losing some of his patience. He is trying to force them to back down without denying the request. “Were you not present for her exam?”

“I wasn’t trying during my exams,” Angelica says, and all eyes turn to her. She looks absolutely terrifying and stunning at the same time. Her lack of coloring makes her look carved from white marble, and equally emotionless.

Slowly she walks up to Victor, and they stare at each other. Minutes go by. Victor cannot stop this now. Finally he starts to circle, but before either can begin, Angelica straightens and looks towards the entrance of the court. I listen, not able to hear anything at first.

After several seconds, it is apparent to all of us that someone is running towards the court. Angelica does not move.

"He is not allowed here," Victor says to Angelica, a barely noticeable tension in his voice.

"I know the rules, Tolken," Angelica states smoothly. "He can go anywhere I go if he believes there is danger. Do you think fighting the Tolken is dangerous?"

Victor does not reply. He cannot answer her and win his argument. Fighting the Tolken is very dangerous if he were fighting at his capacity. Something he would never do against Angelica.

"What are you doing?" Kyle asks, barely out of breath. When did he get so in shape? He ran quite a long way as fast as he could.

"Victor was going to show the Slayers how to fight me," Angelica says neutrally.

Kyle walks to Victor, getting as close as he can without touching him. Kyle is a couple inches taller than Victor and much more muscular. It doesn't look like a fair fight, but everyone in this room except one knows Victor could tear him apart. Kyle will always be blinded by his love and duty to Angelica.

"You would fight a new Guard, a human replacement? Is this how the Tolken proves himself?" Kyle is aflame with anger, not bothering to hide any of it. Angelica's demeanor changes ever so slightly.

"I would fight my Vegar's Votary."

"No, you will not," Kyle says firmly. As long as he is Guard to Angelica, he calls the shots with Victor. In front of these eyes I must stay neutral.

"As you can see, there is no danger here," Victor replies, using his only leverage. Kyle looks at Angelica as if expecting her to come to his side. He must know she will not follow behind him—both of our reputations are on the line. Instead Angelica walks to *my* side. Kyle leaves, and the Slayers return to their training. Victor waits an appropriate amount of time then leaves as well. Shortly after that, Angelica slips away.

Chapter 27

Angelica

Thoughts ramble around my weary mind as I slip through the caves. Is this my life now? An eternity of constantly being torn between Clara and Kyle. If I disregard the four years of lost memories, I've been Lymerian longer than human. And what about the human world? Will they ever let me walk through the grass in my bare feet, feel the sun on my skin, the wind in my hair? I can't imagine going forever without those things.

My feet pause as I reach the edge of the Slayer's cave. I should be with Clara and Vic. He is still there somewhere, my Vic. As I was fighting those Slayers, I could feel a hundred emotions coming from him. I'm not sure what it means, but I know he cares about me. It wasn't all pretend.

Kyle will be waiting for me in our room. The weight of the upcoming argument slows my steps. I need Kyle. I can't begin to imagine how awful life would be without him. But I also need Clara, and she comes with the Slayers and Vic. When I finally walk into the room and see his face, I know all of Krisenica is going to hear his outburst.

"What were you doing with him today? I know it was Clara's idea to show you off to her Slayers, but that does not explain why the Tolken was there." Kyle is sitting on the bed, hands clasped together trying to keep calm.

"How should I know? I'm tired. The Slayers wanted to train with me, and it really wore me out." I go over to him, nuzzling my mouth against his neck. Maybe this will just blow over, and my exhausted body wants blood. He pushes me away and stands.

"You fought them! How many? Why couldn't I tell you were in danger?"

I sigh. No blood for me. I think about finding Jordan until Kyle's anger sweeps into me. I hold my hands up in a peace gesture. "I wasn't in danger. They don't scare me. I had no physical or mental reaction to them." The words seem reasonable to me, but they make him even more upset.

"But you did with him. You panicked for a fraction of a second. I felt it, and I ran. Why would you ever fight the Tolken? He is nearly as strong as Clara and . . . a vicious fighter."

He's right, but it wasn't fear of Vic that startled me. It was my reaction to his fear when he realized he was going to have to fight me.

"Kyle, I have to train with Slayers and Vic. You have to accept that."

Kyle's eyes rage. "There is no Vic. There is only Victor—the Tolken. He doesn't care about you. You have no idea who he truly is. I've seen him slaughter humans, and Merrick was right by his side! Slayers are not like us—they take life and we save it." His words make me flinch. He doesn't say Clara was there too, but I know it's true.

"You trust Clara. She has slaughtered too."

"She is bound by our highest laws to mentor and protect you. I spent years watching her every day, making sure she only had your best interest in mind. She has changed." Kyle sits down on the bed and rests his head in his hands.

"Clara won't let anything happen to me while I'm training. You know that." Slowly I lift my hand to his back and he stills. Twice he takes a deep breath, like he wants to say something but can't. On the third try, his body shudders and chokes out the words.

"You have . . . to release me."

A sharp stab in my heart makes me jump back. If I release Kyle, then I will lose him. Our connection will sever.

"No," I breathe.

"You don't need a Guard—you want a friend. An ally you can trust and lean on."

"That's not true. I need you." My eyes sting with tears as the reality of what he wants settles over me.

"Don't." He wipes his hand across his face and pulls away from my touch. "You have no idea. Every day we are together, every night I lie next to you, I always want more."

"I want more too. You're the one that stops us from going further."

"No, Angelica. I know the human world. I would never . . . do that unless we were really together."

"We are together," I sob, reaching for his hand. Kyle stands, desperate to get away from my touch.

"We are not mates," Kyle says softly. Even as his rigid posture shows confidence that he is right, his eyes are giving me one last chance to take him, to claim him and keep him forever. I can't do it. Something inside of me won't let me. "I can feel your stomach in knots, torn between me and . . ."

"I release you," I whisper. Kyle exhales and his shoulders slump as he turns away from me. With each of his steps, I feel myself go colder and colder until there is nothing left in me but emptiness.

* * *

That night, I dream for the first time in years. Rebecca, Vic, and I are sitting together at a park near the Franklin's house. All three of us are squeezed onto a blanket having a picnic. Vic and I are so close our shoulders touch, and Rebecca sits between our knees. I'm there, but I feel nothing. I don't want to ask Rebecca questions or try to find the answers. I don't want Vic to hold me and make everything go away. I want to leave, to walk away and never come back.

"You are ruining my favorite Franklin memory." My eyes snap open and sweep across the room. I feel an electric charge in the air just before I notice Rebecca. She is sitting on the edge of the bed, just as I remember her though the bed does not bend with her weight.

"What are you doing? How can I see you when you feel far away?"

Rebecca smiles and leans over to me. "I am in your mind. If I actually came to your room, everyone in Mountain Top would know it. It's late now, and almost everyone is sleeping. They won't notice this."

"What do you really look like?" My Rebecca would be nearly thirty, while I spend another eighty years frozen at seventeen.

Rebecca's face slims and her skin tightens around eyes as white as Etherial's. Her beautiful blonde hair darkens as it shrinks into a pixie cut. She looks like a teenage version of Rebecca except for the black hair and shining eyes. Is this the little girl I loved? If she were in danger, would I still respond as before? I lay back down and turn onto my side. My body feels cold and sick without Kyle near.

"This pain will pass in time, just as it did when you moved on from me and Vic." Rebecca can still read me like a book, but my other sense tells me she's hiding something. "You still have Clara."

"I thought Clara would have come," I say, not even trying to hide my sadness.

"She is blocking you. Since the moment the four of you came out of the dungeons, she became the Vegar again. The Vegar must keep a clear head at all times, which means removing herself emotionally from you." Even Rebecca is in awe of Clara—adoration flows from her.

"Why are you here, Rebecca?"

"I watch you a lot. Tonight is the first night you've spent alone since you left the cell." I know it should matter to me that Rebecca came as soon as it was safe to, but I feel nothing.

"Thank you for what you did in the arena. Being a Litmar would have been terrible. Thank you for checking on me now, but I think you should go."

"I came here to help you find Merrick."

Now I feel something. With Lymerian speed, I'm out of bed and next to Rebecca.

"How can I find him?" My senses are on full alert.

"You track him, of course. Merrick's blood is forever a part of you; it will lead you to him."

Merrick. I force myself to think of Merrick and our short time together. The taste of his blood comes back to me, and I feel him. His weak heartbeat thumps in my ears.

"How far away is he?"

"Close. The Litmars will keep him close until his first grandchild is born."

"How can I get out of here?

"I'm going to let you out. I have enough strength to get you through the mountain. From there you must hurry. Clara will find you and make you come back." Rebecca turns her head to one of the walls and a light grows there. I can see rocks and trees.

I jump through the wall. Then I run.

Excitement pulses through my blood as I get closer and closer to the answers I've been waiting fifteen years to find out. The fresh air, cool grass, and hard earth can wait. There is no time to marvel in freedom.

Following Merrick's blood leads me to a ranch home sitting unprotected in the middle of an open range. I stop at the edge of the clearing and listen. The house is dark but full of sound. I hear more than his heartbeat. Children. I take a deep breath because I know I can't go in. There's no telling what I'll do when I see him.

"Merrick!" I shout.

The house stays black, but I hear the creak of floorboards under light steps. Eventually the back door opens.

Merrick looks so much older than I remember. Time has gone by for him, finally. Though I do not age, I am nearly unrecognizable. Merrick, heart beating fast, looks back into the house before pulling the door shut behind him. Our eyes meet and I charge, legs pumping hard. Then I hit a brick wall.

Chapter 28

Clara

Thoughts of the future plague me for the rest of the evening. I cannot sleep, so I lay awake staring at the ceiling. Kyle is already holding Angelica back—she must release him. Yet having Kyle's love and protection is the one thing she knows she can count on. If she knew the entire truth of her Liturgy, she would feel differently. She would not hesitate to release Kyle. The air in the room begins a familiar buzz around me.

Rebecca. Her form appears at the edge of the room. She is still hiding herself in a child's body.

"Why are you here?" I ask, looking back toward the ceiling.

"You need to go." I stand straight up at her words—she is still an Astro. I move close to examine the Rebecca I see in this room. She is not really here; I cannot touch her. Somehow the Astros can project things through space, even themselves.

"What have you done?" I close my eyes and track Angelica. She is no longer in Krisenica. Rebecca must have done something to prevent me from recognizing Angelica's escape the moment it happened.

"She may have forgiven all of us, but she still blames Merrick. I have watched and waited for five years and her heart is still full of hate for him. I do not want her to hate him. I let her go so that she could make her peace with Merrick." My heart starts to race as terror seizes me. Angelica cannot be in the human world, and Merrick is not far from Krisenica. She will reach him before I can stop her.

"Did it ever occur to you that she might kill him?" Rebecca flinches. "Please tell me you looked down this path before you sent her on it."

Rebecca looks away. "Not all of us believe in searching futures. I do not invade another's privacy unless I am ordered to."

"Then do it," I command, knowing the Laws of Liturgy bind her to it. Rebecca's eyes brighten as they move wildly from side to side.

"Leave now," Rebecca recites in a flat tone.

"What is going on?" Victor's eyes shift from me to Rebecca. I grab his arm and pull him towards the exit.

"Clara, wait." I freeze, my heart pounding loud enough for anyone near us to hear. "When you reach her, you must make her remember." It is an order, one I do not think I can ignore. A moment later she is gone, and we dart from the room.

"Rebecca let her out," I explain quietly as we make our way out of the caves. Already my mind is coordinating how to exit Krisenica without attracting attention. Victor goes tense, his heart rate now matching mine.

Krisenica has many exits in case we are attacked. Slipping out in the middle of the night is easiest. There is no time to explain, so we must choose an exit where we will not be discovered.

We make for the elevator that goes to Mountain Top. Normally this elevator is locked unless you have business with the Astros. I am counting on Rebecca to have the door unlocked since it is our best chance to leave unnoticed.

It is open. The elevator will take us far in the mountains where no one is keeping watch. Then we will jump off the mountain and run like hell.

"I told you Rebecca was trouble," I say as we wait for the elevator to reach the top. "This could be catastrophic."

"I thought you trusted the Astros."

"Rebecca is not behaving like an Astro. She said she does not believe in looking into futures unless she is ordered. What kind of Astros believes in that? That is the point of being an Astro!"

The elevator stops before he can reply. The moment the doors open enough to fit our bodies, we run. We move as fast as our limbs can take us, building more and more speed until the drop off. Hitting the correct distance for the jump is not the problem—it is landing without breaking anything.

My body leaps through the air, and it feels like I'm falling forever. My speed increases as I drop. With less than a hundred feet to go, Victor appears underneath me, slowing my decent. Just before we land, I jump from him. All four of my limbs touch down at once, and I roll forward until I gain enough control to stand.

"That was not necessary!" I shout to him as I start running. He ignores me.

The clearing is short, quickly feeding into more woods. I hear Victor beside me, going over and around the trees. We are keeping up with each other. Merrick's home is only twenty miles from Krisenica. The quickest path is through these dense woods. Twenty minutes later both of us burst from the trees just in time.

Chapter 29

Angelica

"No!" Clara shouts. She and Vic have their arms tightly around me. Merrick stays ten feet away from our struggle. I nearly made it to the front steps.

"Angelica, stop struggling. You cannot fight through both of us," Vic says. "We will drag you the twenty miles back to Krisenica if we have to. I thought you could make her stop," he snaps to Clara.

Reluctantly, Clara says stop and the fight leaves me instantly—though my rage at Merrick still simmers just beneath the surface. The four of us stare at each other. But no, Merrick is not staring at me, the girl he sacrificed for himself, or Victor, his best friend—he is staring at Clara.

"I am sorry it was you," Merrick says softly.

"That is unlikely. This is exactly how you wanted it," Clara replies coldly, taking a step away from Merrick. Merrick starts to reply, but then turns to me, finally taking inventory.

"She looks like old Lymerians. How strange," he whispers. "You were right all along, Victor."

"No. She is a Guard, an incredibly strong one."

"I'm right here!" I shout, cutting Victor off. "Does it matter what I look like? Is that all you have to say!" I scream at him, wishing I could drag my nails down his back. Clara's command is keeping me firmly in place. "I died for you!"

"And what life did you leave behind?" Merrick asks, his face right next to mine and without fear now that Clara and Victor are here. "Your beloved life was not real. The only real thing about your life was that pathetic human you called a friend."

Even Clara's command cannot hold me after Merrick's harsh words about my only true friend—Janice. My fisted hand buries itself in his stomach while my opposite arm swipes an elbow across his face an instant later. Merrick drops as Victor moves between us, his hands locking around my arms and waist quicker than lightning strikes. Clara moves as well, in front of Merrick. He is on the ground, gasping.

"You don't know!" I shout. "You don't know what life I would have had with my real family. All of you took it from me!" Vic's grip on me tightens, making it hard for me to breathe, but I still struggle to get free.

As soon as Clara is sure Victor will not let me go, she bends down to Merrick, leaning her head against his. "Are you okay?" She gently checks him over.

Merrick laughs and then yelps a little in pain when she touches his stomach. "I am fine. Not a life-threatening injury, even for a human."

Clara starts to back away from him, but he grabs her arm.

"I miss you, more than you can imagine. My anger with you died that night in the arena."

For a split second, I do not understand the love and desperation in his voice. Then my heart drops as everything falls into place. The final piece of the puzzle.

Clara's head snaps to me. Everything I need to know is written in her eyes.

Merrick was the mate Clara lost before I came to Kresenica.

Victor's arms flex even tighter around me. "Clara, she is going to lose it. We have to get her back to Krisenica. Where are Jordan and Kyle? They should be here by now. Guards are not this slow."

"Clara, if you cannot control her . . ." Merrick says, his voice further away. Finally, he is afraid. He is inching back to the house.

I snarl at him and strain against Vic's arms. I can't let him get away. "If you live through this, you will know how I feel the moment they steal your grandchild."

Merrick shakes his head with a small smile, looking at me as if I'm an idiot child. "No, I will not. Just as was done to your grandfather and parents, my memories will be erased. When that child is born, I will truly be free."

It's too much and Victor knows it. He squeezes me harder, threatening to break the bones in my arms, but I don't think even that can stop me. In an instant, I break his forearms and flash toward Merrick.

"No," Clara says firmly, but she has no power over me. "Remember!" she shouts, and my body hesitates. Clara is suddenly between Merrick and me, and somehow I have stopped. She takes my face in her hands. Her black eyes pierce me as she says, "Remember Merrick, remember Victor . . . remember me."

Remember

Book 2 of The Replacement Series

Coming in 2019

ABOUT THE AUTHOR

Bianca has been writing stories since she was a little girl, and it has remained her favorite hobby. In 2006, she graduated from Western Illinois University with a BA in Elementary Education. In 2012, she switched career paths and began working in the public library system. Later that year, she graduated from Clarion University with a MA in Library Science. Currently, Bianca is a branch manager for the Davenport Public Library in Davenport, Iowa.

Online she is known as Bianca LibLady, with a YouTube channel and website dedicated to teen interests. Her website offers book suggestions, seasonal tips, TV blogs, an author page and more.

Bianca plays French horn in the Quad City Wind Ensemble. Exercise, baking, and reading are among her favorite hobbies. She and her husband live in Iowa with their three children.

www.biancaliblady.com

Made in the USA
San Bernardino, CA
17 October 2018